" 'NO TRUE KLINGON WOULD BETRAY HIS WORD OF HONOR,' " ME-LARR QUOTED.

"When you told me that, Captain Klag, did you lie?"

"No. It was, however, a mistake."

"You said it was the most important tenet of your people!"

Te-Run, oldest and wisest of the Ruling Pack, said, "Then we are to be conquered."

"No," Klag said, "the *Gorkon* will defend your world to the last dying breath of each warrior on board. Other Klingons may be willing to turn their backs on honor, but I am not."

STAR TREK®

I.K.S.
GORKON

BOOK TWO

HONOR BOUND

Keith R.A. DeCandido

**Based upon STAR TREK® and
STAR TREK: THE NEXT GENERATION®
created by Gene Roddenberry**

POCKET BOOKS
New York   London   Toronto   Sydney   Singapore

This book is a work of fiction. Names, characters, places and incidents are products of the author's imagination or are used fictitiously. Any resemblance to actual events or locales or persons, living or dead, is entirely coincidental.

An Original Publication of POCKET BOOKS

POCKET BOOKS, a division of Simon & Schuster, Inc.
1230 Avenue of the Americas, New York, NY 10020

STAR TREK is a Registered Trademark of Paramount Pictures.

This book is published by Pocket Books, a division of Simon & Schuster, Inc., under exclusive license from Paramount Pictures.

ISBN: 0-7434-5716-1

First Pocket Books printing December 2003

10 9 8 7 6 5 4 3 2 1

POCKET and colophon are registered trademarks of Simon & Schuster, Inc.

Manufactured in the United States of America

For information regarding special discounts for bulk purchases, please contact Simon & Schuster Special Sales at 1-800-456-6798 or business@simonandschuster.com

For Marc Okrand, who told us how they speak,
Ronald D. Moore, who told us how they live,
and Michael Dorn, who showed us who they are

It is the purpose that makes strong the vow,
But vows to every purpose must not hold.

—William Shakespeare, *Troilus and Cressida*,
Act 5, scene 3, lines 23–24

HISTORIAN'S NOTE

This novel immediately follows Book 1 of this series, *A Good Day to Die*. It takes place approximately eight and a half months after *Star Trek: Deep Space Nine*'s final episode, "What You Leave Behind," and about three years prior to the movie *Star Trek Nemesis*. That would put it at the end of the Year of Kahless 1001 on the Klingon calendar, at approximately Stardate 53800 on the Starfleet calendar, and in late 2376 on the human calendar.

HONOR BOUND

PROLOGUE

"I am Klag, son of M'Raq, captain of the *I.K.S. Gorkon*—and I summon you, my fellow members of the Order of the *Bat'leth*, in a call to honor.

"When the Order was first formed, by the Lady Lukara after Kahless's ascension to *Sto-Vo-Kor*, its members were tasked with ensuring that the teachings of the divine one would continue after the teacher was gone—to make sure that the Great Houses of the Klingon Empire remained on the path of honor, and to lead them back to that path if ever they strayed. Chancellor Martok has, in his wisdom, returned the Order to that original sacred purpose, and it is for such that I summon you now.

"Ten weeks ago, a dozen ships, including the *Gorkon*, were sent to the Kavrot Sector to find new worlds on which to plant the Klingon flag. A week ago, the *Gorkon* found one, in the system designated

Kavrot *loSmaH Soch*. Called San-Tarah by its native population, the world's orbit is littered with subspace eddies. We have determined that it is the fallout from a battle with subspace weapons fought some time within the last two centuries. These eddies have played havoc with our technologies, hindering some, eliminating others. Energy weapons do not function on or near San-Tarah, and communications only in the short range. However, the planet itself is rich with such mineral resources as kellinite, koltanium, and uridium—it would make a glorious addition to the Empire.

"The native population is a warrior culture. You may think that makes them like us, but they are different—the planet is *so* abundant that they can afford a pure warrior ethic that Kahless himself would envy. The day-to-day compromises of life do not affect them. When we first beamed ground troops down, we surprised them, arriving at night by a method of transport far beyond their means—and still they succeeded in driving us from their village.

"I had planned to beam down a larger force and take them, but then the leader of their Ruling Pack requested an audience. They wished to discuss how the battle might continue. They did *not* wish to speak of peace—in fact, the translator did not render the word *peace* into one that they could comprehend. No, they were only interested in how best to continue fighting, for they, like we, value battle above all else.

"I learned something, speaking with the head of

their Ruling Pack, a wise and powerful warrior named Me-Larr: We would not defeat the Children of San-Tarah. Oh, we might very well crush them, we could easily overtake them even with our curtailed weapons capability, but they would defy us from the oldest warrior to the youngest cub.

"They also offered us an alternative. They proposed five martial contests. If we defeated them in the majority of these contests, they would willingly cede themselves to the Klingon Empire. If they defeated us, we would go and never trouble their world again.

"I looked into Me-Larr's heart when he made this offer. I knew that these were honorable foes—more, they were *worthy* ones. And so I agreed.

"In the end, we were defeated. More specifically, *I* was. We bested them in the hunt and in a seek-and-capture combat mission, while they got the better of us in marine combat and in a one-to-one contest of strength. In the end, it was left to me and my *bat'leth* to face Me-Larr and his sword. After many hours of glorious battle, I was finally defeated. Though Me-Larr spared my life, he did declare a just victory, which I conceded to him. I gave him my word that I would honor our agreement, and that the Klingon Empire would leave these fine warriors to their own planet.

"Only a few minutes ago, I received this message from General Talak."

"*Captain Klag, I have reviewed your reports. While I appreciate your admiration for these primitives, I do not appreciate your attempts to speak on the Empire's behalf, nor do I see any reason for the future of the Empire to be governed by words spoken to those who deserve only to be jeghpu'wI'. Regardless of the outcome of this ridiculous 'contest' that you and these people have concocted, San-Tarah is a world that must come under our flag. Brenlek will be fully conquered within three days of your reception of this message. You are to hold station at San-Tarah and await the arrival of the task force in five days' time. I expect a full map of the subspace eddies and a tactical analysis of how best to secure the planet given the limitations presented by those eddies by the time the fleet arrives. San-Tarah will become part of the Empire within the next two weeks. I will contact you again when the task force is en route. Out."*

"Is *this* now the face of the Empire? Are we no longer Klingons? Do we break vows at a whim, ignore promises that inconvenience us? I say we do not. Kahless slew his own brother because that brother went back on his word. I am a Klingon warrior, a proud member of the Order of the *Bat'leth*, and captain of one of our warships—if I do not speak for the Empire, then who does?

"General Talak is sending his fleet to this system in order to conquer a people to whom I have sworn the Empire's protection. I would not be worthy of my position as captain nor of my induction into the Order if I did not defy the general. I do not take this action because I wish to—for I have no desire to engage my fellow Klingons in battle—but because I *must*. If we allow this to happen, then all we fought

4

for against the Dominion will have been lost. We are not mindless Jem'Hadar who blindly obey our Vorta handlers. We are *Klingons*—we are *warriors!* And we must stand against this atrocity before it has a chance to spread!

"Join me—bring the Empire back to glory. The days of such honorless behavior must be put in the past forever!"

Klag ended the recording, encoded it onto a data spike, and sat back in his chair. He had the support of his first officer, Commander Kornan. Now he needed to go out to the bridge and secure the support of his crew. He had little doubt that he would get it; he had been in command for over half a year, and knew that the warriors of the *Gorkon* were among the finest in the Defense Force.

The true test was the call to the Order. Would they heed Martok's return to the Order's primary function? Even if they did, would they consider this a fulfillment of that mandate?

If not, Klag thought, *I will be one ship against many.* Talak's fleet included a dozen ships, though he might well leave a few behind at Brenlek.

And then there is Dorrek. Just as Klag had found San-Tarah, Klag's estranged younger brother Dorrek had found Brenlek as commander of the *I.K.S. K'mpec.* Klag would not be at all surprised if the *K'mpec*—a massive warship of the same class as the *Gorkon*—accompanied Talak's fleet.

Like Kahless, I too may need to take up arms against

my sibling. So be it. Dorrek had never forgiven Klag for refusing to see their father, M'Raq, when he chose to wait for death on the Homeworld rather than reclaim the honor he lost when he was captured by Romulans. Nor had his younger brother thought any better of Klag when he chose, shortly after M'Raq died in his sleep, to have their father's right arm grafted onto Klag's own shoulder to replace the one he had lost during the war. Dorrek had refused to acknowledge Klag's supremacy as older brother, so Klag would treat him as any other honorless *petaQ*.

M'Raq's arm was a few centimeters shorter than that of his eldest son. As a result, Klag—despite having several months to grow accustomed to the new limb—still often listed to the right whenever he got up out of a chair. He did so again now, cursing as he stumbled rightward, grateful that Kornan had left the office moments before he began his recording for his fellow members of the Order.

He went onto the bridge and played the general's message for the crew. A breach of protocol, perhaps—the words of generals to captains were not usually fit for the eyes of mere crew to see—but it was best for them to hear the reasons for what he was about to ask of them unfiltered.

To his relief, but not his surprise, the crew was behind him. "Strike them down!" one cried. "We go with honor!" said another.

Then the second officer, Lieutenant Toq, led them in song—an old victory chant called "Don't

Speak." Klag smiled as he joined in the titular refrain of "*yIja'Qo', yIja'Qo', yIja'Qo'.*" Their song was sung throughout the halls of the mighty vessel.

After the second verse, cheers echoed off the bridge's bulkheads. Toq and the substitute gunner, Grint, head-butted.

"Fear not!" Klag cried over the din. When he spoke, the bridge grew quiet again. "We will not face the honorless general alone. Over a thousand years ago, the Order of the *Bat'leth* was formed after Kahless ascended to *Sto-Vo-Kor*—both to spread his word and to enforce his doctrine. Today, the call will go out once more. Again, the Order of the *Bat'leth* will serve to remind the galaxy of what it means to be a Klingon!"

Klag walked over to Toq and handed him the spike onto which he had recorded his message and his Order of the *Bat'leth* medallion. Indicating the medallion, he said, "This will allow you to send a tight-beam communication to anyone else in the Order." Then he held up the spike. "I want you to send the message encoded on this."

Now, he thought after Toq took both items, *we wait. . . .*

CHAPTER ONE

Captain K'Vada watched as Klag's face faded from the small viewscreen. He then removed the Order of the *Bat'leth* medallion from his workstation, and was about to put it back in the drawer from which he'd retrieved it only a few minutes before. Just before he did, he hesitated, then decided to put the medallion at its proper place on his shoulder. *It's been too long since I wore it. Longer still since wearing it actually meant anything.*

K'Vada's service to the Empire went back to his youth—a youth that went back fairly far, much as he hated to admit it. He had won many campaigns, brought honor to his House, and continued to grow older. Eventually, he knew, he would slow down, and some ambitious first officer would decide to challenge him. Or perhaps a worthy foe would send him to *Sto-Vo-Kor*—though if the Romulan, Federation, Kinshaya, Kreel, Dominion, Cardassian, and Breen foes he'd faced over the years couldn't manage it, K'Vada didn't see how anyone else would. He had never considered himself to be an especially great warrior, yet here he was, still fighting after all these years, after all these campaigns.

With the decommissioning of his previous command following the war, he had only recently taken command of the *I.K.S. Vidd.* The previous captain had been the victim of a duel relating to some family feud or other. K'Vada came from a minor House that had never offended anyone; it was not of enough consequence to do so. As a result, his life had been refreshingly free of such distractions.

Unfortunately, Command placed him in charge rather than promoting the first officer, Commander Vigh. *His* House was of considerable consequence, which explained his high rank; his incompetence was also considerable, which explained K'Vada's placement on the ship over him. But it also meant that K'Vada needed to watch his back.

Entering the bridge, he saw that Vigh was sitting in the command chair. Although there was no regulation prohibiting it, Defense Force tradition held that no one save the ship's supreme commander sat in that chair, regardless of who was in command of the bridge. K'Vada supposed that Vigh could have come up with a more obvious insult, but one didn't readily spring to mind.

As the door to his office rumbled closed behind him, K'Vada said, "Pilot, change course to the

Kavrot Sector, system *loSmaH Soch,* maximum warp."

Vigh, K'Vada noticed, did not rise from the command chair. "Sir, we have been assigned to patrol this sector for the next three days."

As if I did not know that. "We have new orders."

"No communications have arrived from Command."

This was, strictly speaking, true. The message from Klag came on a tight-beam subspace carrier wave that bypassed the *Vidd*'s communications system and went straight to K'Vada's Order medallion. K'Vada did not respond directly to Vigh's statement, but instead turned back to the pilot. "Is the course laid in?"

"Yes, sir."

"Execu—"

Vigh rose from the command chair. "Belay that!"

K'Vada sighed. *I should have known.* "Pilot, execute at maximum warp, or I will replace you with a living officer who understands the chain of command." He turned to Vigh. "That goes for you as well, Commander."

"We have received no change in our orders!"

"*We* have not. *I* have." Indicating the Order medallion, K'Vada added, "This is official business of the Order of the *Bat'leth,* which supersedes any authority save that of the emperor himself."

To K'Vada's satisfaction, the pilot engaged the warp drive as soon as K'Vada mentioned the Order.

Whereupon Vigh unsheathed his *d'k tahg,* the secondary blades unfurling with a dual click. The captain sighed.

"It was not enough that Command did not give me this ship that was rightfully mine, but to put a lying sack of *taknar* droppings in my place is an insult I will bear no longer! The *Vidd* will be *mine!*"

K'Vada contemplated wasting his breath pointing out the rightness of his position with regard to the Order, but decided against it, choosing to simply unsheathe his own personal dagger. Vigh was making use of these events as an excuse to finally challenge K'Vada. *Better to get this challenge out in the open and over with than to let it fester on the bridge for months on end.*

"Now," Vigh continued, "you will be exposed for the honorless *petaQ* you trul—"

His diatribe was cut off by K'Vada slashing at his face.

Vigh stumbled backward, apparently surprised that K'Vada didn't wait until he was done giving his speech before attacking. Blood seeped from the wound in his cheek.

Screaming, Vigh lunged forward in a clumsy attack that K'Vada easily sidestepped. He had an opportunity to strike back, but decided against it. K'Vada hadn't had a good workout in far too long.

Within five minutes, it was clear he wasn't going to get one now, either. What Vigh lacked in command competence, he more than made up for in clumsiness. His attacks were the tiresomely predictable ones of a novice fighter. K'Vada had seen children fresh off their first hunt wield a *d'k tahg* with more skill than his soon-to-be-former first officer.

Finally, on Vigh's fourth obvious lunge, K'Vada again sidestepped, and plunged his own *d'k tahg* right into Vigh's chest. *I should have done this weeks ago.*

By this time, the entire complement of the bridge was chanting K'Vada's name. He removed the dagger and let Vigh's body fall to the deck. The captain then moved to the command chair, not bothering with the death ritual. That was only for honored warriors bound for *Sto-Vo-Kor*, a state of affairs that most assuredly did *not* apply to Vigh.

The second officer—now the first officer—grinned and said, "You have done a great service to this vessel today, Captain."

"I did nothing that Vigh did not bring upon himself," K'Vada said dismissively as he sat in his chair and saw the distorted starfield on the viewscreen that indicated that they were at warp. "Pilot, time to destination?"

"Twenty-seven hours, sir."

"Speak with engineering about increasing engine efficiency. I want us at that star system as soon as possible."

Stepping around from the operations console to K'Vada's side, the new first officer—Lieutenant Yivogh—spoke in a low voice, so their conversation would only be heard by the two of them. "Sir, may I know our new mission?"

"We go into battle to preserve the honor of our

Empire, *Commander*," he said, making it clear that an elevation in rank went with the elevation in position, prompting a grin from Yivogh. "You will know more when the time is right."

"As you command, sir."

K'Vada nodded, and leaned back in his chair. *Not a bad morning*, he thought. First what appeared to be a call to glory. Then he rid himself of his burdensome first officer—which, judging by the crew's reaction, would serve only to solidify his own position as captain. Yivogh might have had ambitions of his own, of course, and he was as likely as not to view the peculiar nature of this mission as an opportunity for advancement, much as his predecessor had.

For now, however, he is grateful to me, and I will use that for as long as I may. And then, Klag, we shall see if your call to glory is true. . . .

Bekk Maris sat in his new bunk on the *Gorkon*, reading *Warriors of the Deep Winter*, the latest novel by K'Ratak. It was disappointing. There was a time when a new release from the novelist was a cause for celebration. Maris still remembered the day that *The Vision of Judgment*, the long-awaited sequel to *The Dream of Fire*, was released. He had arranged to have no duties to perform on that day, and spent all of it reading the new book. He finished it that day, and reread it, but it had not been the transcendent experience that the first one had been. Now, six books later, Maris was forced to admit that *The Dream of*

Fire was not just K'Ratak's greatest work, but his only good one. The author was, in Maris's considered opinion, coasting on the reputation of that one bit of genius.

Maris wasn't the only one who felt that way. An irate reader had met K'Ratak at a public appearance and challenged him, saying he was no longer worthy of his accolades. However, to the irritation of many dissatisfied readers, K'Ratak won the duel handily, and no one had dared challenge him since.

Looking up from his reading, Maris surveyed his new surroundings. In truth, they were no different from his old surroundings: a bunk, two meters in length, one meter in width, and half a meter in height, the same as assigned to each of the fifteen hundred soldiers on the *Gorkon.* The difference was that he was now in the top bunk belonging to Fifteenth Squad instead of the middle one belonging to the seventh.

It had all begun last night when he returned from dinner to find that his belongings had been removed.

"You're in the wrong place, *Bekk.*"

Maris had turned to see Avok, the Leader of the seventh. As usual, the Leader's hair was flying in all directions, his beard untended, with bits of the evening meal's *bok-rat* liver amid the hairs.

"What's going on, Avok?"

"It seems that the entire eighteenth has been promoted to the seventh. *QaS DevwI'* Vok was impressed with their performance during the initial attack on San-Tarah."

Scowling, Maris said, "The *entire* eighteenth? All four?" Avok nodded. "But what of me? And Trant?" The other two members of the seventh had been killed during one of the contests against the San-Tarah.

"According to Lieutenant Lokor, you've both been transferred to fill the two spots in the fifteenth."

Angrily, Maris asked, "Why have we been demoted?" Maris knew that the fifteenth, too, had lost a pair of soldiers to the San-Tarah, but that didn't explain why the ranks were being filled with superior soldiers. A post on one of the finest new warships in the fleet was a great honor, as was an assignment to the seventh. The *Gorkon* had three hundred five-soldier squads, and to be among the first fifteen of those—under the general command of *QaS DevwI'* Vok—was a great privilege. To have that privilege— well, not revoked as such, but at least diminished did not sit at all well with Maris.

Avok smiled, showing a mouth full of gaps between too-rare instances of teeth. "You'll have to ask Lieutenant Lokor. I just do what they tell me."

That's always Avok's excuse, Maris thought. Aloud, he simply said, "I see."

"Leader Wol is waiting for you at the fifteenth's bunks."

Oh no. Oh no no no. Now it all made sense to Maris.

Before their arrival at San-Tarah, Trant and Maris had gotten into a fight. Maris couldn't even remember what it was about—they were both just aggravated by the enforced inactivity of nine weeks of useless exploration of the Kavrot Sector. The second officer, Lieutenant Toq, had broken up the fight, along with Leader Wol of the fifteenth. Wol had convinced Toq not to report their brawl to the *QaS DevwI'* or to Lokor, for which Maris, at least, was grateful, but Toq's price for that was to make Maris and Trant's subsequent behavior Wol's responsibility.

It seems that it is to be taken literally now. Resigned to the inevitable, Maris made his way to the fifteenth's bunks.

Without thinking, he got into the middle bunk, assuming that he would occupy the same spot. However, the quartermaster had either not bothered to keep the same alignment, or simply didn't care. When Maris went to retrieve his personal padd, he found that they had put Trant's belongings in the middle bunk.

A few minutes later, Maris climbed to the topmost bunk, and found his own items there.

After a night's sleep, he awoke and tried to finish off *Warriors* when he heard footsteps approaching. He looked up to see Trant, walking stiffly. "I see that B'Oraq has finally freed you from your prison."

Trant's legs had been shredded by one of the alien creatures on the planet below. They appeared to have healed, but B'Oraq had, typically, insisted he remain in the medical bay overnight, as if a biobed were a proper place for a soldier. Trant was as proud a warrior as you could find, and might have made a fine officer. Apparently, though, his way was blocked.

When they were assigned to the *Gorkon* together months ago, Trant had told Maris: "The sons of petty criminals do not become officers."

"Yes," he said now in reply to Maris's comment. "Our *yIntagh* of a doctor warned me that I would have 'difficulty' walking. She also said she was going to recommend I remain shipboard for the time being." He scowled. "I believe she meant that as a joke."

Maris grinned. "It is hard to tell with her. She learned medicine in the Federation, remember—I believe she has picked up their peculiar sense of humor."

"Perhaps." He gazed dolefully at the bunks. "Lieutenant Toq had better hope that we do not encounter each other away from prying eyes."

Maris barked a laugh. "Speak a little louder, fool. Perhaps Lokor will hear you and kill you once and for all."

Another voice said, "Lokor wouldn't waste his time on such sputum as yourselves."

Looking past Trant, Maris saw Leader Wol approaching the bunk area, along with G'joth, an old *bekk* with waist-length white hair and a horn-shaped beard, and the infamous *Bekk* Goran, by far the largest and strongest Klingon on the *Gorkon*—and, perhaps, in the Defense Force. He towered over the other two by a full head.

"And he won't need to," Wol said. "Because I will kill you long before he even has the chance to if given the slightest provocation. You were assigned to the fifteenth because *I* requested it. Toq made me responsible for you, and I take my responsibilities *very* seriously."

"This is madness!" Trant spit on the deck. "We are warriors of the seventh. To be sent to the fifteenth is—"

"Fitting." Wol smiled nastily as she said it. *At least this Leader has all her teeth*, Maris thought with amusement.

"I disagree," G'joth said. "I was hoping for *worthy* replacements for Davok and Krevor, not these two *petaQ.*"

Trant advanced on the *bekk.* "You dare!"

Goran also advanced, his massive form looming over Trant. "If you touch my friend G'joth, I will break you in two, Trant."

Trant ceased his advance. Goran had held a superdense koltanium rock on his back for over seven hours on San-Tarah. He truly could break Trant into two separate pieces if he put his mind to it, and Maris was glad to see that his comrade wasn't foolish enough to put that to the test.

"This is *Bekk* G'joth," Wol said, indicating the white-haired man, "and this is *Bekk* Goran. They are part of the fifteenth. If you're lucky, Trant, you and Maris will live long enough to understand what that means."

"If *we're* lucky," G'joth added, "you won't."

With a sneer, Trant said, "I already know what it means, G'joth—that we are being punished for nothing!"

Wol moved in close enough so that her nose was almost touching Trant's crest. "Oh no, Trant. Not nothing. After your pathetic display near the armory last week, you could very easily have been demoted to the three hundredth and given waste-extraction duty. Instead, you have been given a chance at redemption."

"With *you?*" Again, Trant sneered.

"We held the road at the San-Tarah's Prime Village. We defended the prize in the third contest. Davok and Krevor died with honor. You and Maris have a chance to be a part of that—or you can die a fool's death. The choice is yours. But make it quickly—because if you are to prove worthy, I want to know, and if you aren't I want you dead so we can put someone more deserving in your place."

With that, Wol turned her back on Trant and walked away. Goran and G'joth followed her, also with their backs to him.

Maris laughed. "You should've just gotten into your bunk and kept your mouth shut. It worked for me."

Trant said nothing in response.

The Ruling Pack surrounded Klag, lying on their stomachs in a circle inside what they called their Meeting Hut. The walls of the hut were decorated with the heads of *san-reak*—massive game animals that lived on a distant island. Once a year, shortly before winter, selected members of the Children of San-Tarah hunted this animal, one of which was enough to feed the populace for the entire cold season. The heads—which by themselves were almost larger than a Klingon child—were mounted on the walls as trophies of Great Hunts past.

All fourteen members of the Ruling Pack lay before Klag. The colors of the fur that covered each of the be-snouted bipeds ranged from as white as the snow on Rura Penthe to as black as space, with several variations of brown, gray, and dark red in between. They wore no clothing—their fur was more than adequate protection from the elements, and until Klag's first ground troops beamed to the surface a week ago, they had not known of the concept of body armor. Though it was sometimes difficult to read alien species, Klag was quite certain that they were each looking upon him with a combination of anger and confusion.

Klag had requested the audience with Me-Larr after sending out the call to the Order. Talak's fleet would not arrive for five days. Klag had no idea what results he would get from his summons, if any, but in the meantime, he owed it to Me-Larr's people to inform them of what had happened.

Me-Larr had been angry when Klag transported down, since the captain had sworn an oath not to set foot on San-Tarah again, but that display was as nothing compared with the fury he exhibited when Klag finished telling the story of Talak's betrayal of Klingon honor. He rose and began to pace the length of the hut. The other members of the Ruling Pack seemed equally restless, but remained in their prone state.

"You told me, Captain Klag, that no true Klingon

would betray your word of honor. You told me that your people valued honor above all else. Was that a lie?"

"No. It was, however, a mistake."

"A *mistake?*" Me-Larr's eyes burned with fury; saliva dripped from his teeth. "You said it was the most important tenet of your people!"

"We are not a monolithic species, Me-Larr. We aspire to certain ideals, laid down by Kahless fifteen hundred years ago. It is, however, much easier to aspire than achieve. General Talak has had more difficulty making that journey than I had previously thought."

Te-Run, the oldest and wisest of the Ruling Pack, said, "Then the events of the past few days were for naught. We are to be conquered."

"Not if I have anything to say about it," Klag said. "The *Gorkon* will defend your world to the last dying breath of each warrior on board. General Talak may be willing to turn his back on honor, but I will not."

Another of the Ruling Pack—Ga-Tror, whom Klag knew was their Fight Leader—said, "How many of these ships does General Talak command?"

Technically, as Chancellor Martok's chief of staff, he commanded all of them, but Klag saw no reason to get into that. "His present fleet numbers twelve, possibly thirteen, but they will not all be sent here. Even so, there will be at least two ships and possibly more that are the equal of the *Gorkon.*"

Over the days, Klag had begun to get a grasp of the San-Tarah's body language, so he knew that Ga-Tror's turning his eyes away from Klag now was a decided insult. "Then your defense of our planet would seem to be lacking, Captain Klag."

For his part, Klag looked right at the Fight Leader. "If I were alone, that would be so, but I am not. Even now, ships from throughout the Klingon Empire are wending their way to this star system to come to our aid." Strictly speaking, he did not know this for sure, but he needed to reassure them that his fight on their behalf would be more than a suicidal gesture—*even though it may well be that in the end*, he thought bitterly. "We have also been studying the subspace eddies."

"This is what blocks the stars from our view?" another of the Pack asked.

"Yes. We have begun to find ways to make our weapons and other tools work properly amidst the eddies, and this is not intelligence we will share with our enemies." He looked at each member of the Ruling Pack one by one as he spoke, finally resting his eyes on Me-Larr. "The road to victory will not be an easy one. But I swear to you that the road will be paved with the blood of the honorless cowards who would betray everything that has made the Klingon Empire great. I know you to be among the finest warriors I have ever seen. Those who serve under me have sworn to die defending your planet. I ask now that you join us in doing so. Talak will send troops to the surface—you must be ready for them."

"You can be assured that we will be." The fury had not left Me-Larr's voice. "I told you that we would not surrender to invaders, and we still will not. If this General Talak is to take San-Tarah from us, he must pry it from our dead claws."

Klag smiled. "Good. As I said, you will not be alone. I wish to send our own ground troops down, to fight alongside your people against the troops Talak will send. He will not be prepared for fighters of your caliber, nor for Klingon warriors who have honor *on* their side."

The head of the Ruling Pack went to one corner of the Hut. One of the San-Tarah's odd two-bladed swords hung from a strap on the wall. The blade curved sharply, first angling out from the hilt and then around into a deep crescent. The blade split in two, one going straight upward, the other continuing to form the rest of the crescent. Each blade ended in a V formation. It was with just such a sword that Me-Larr had defeated Klag—armed with a *bat'leth*—in the final contest just a day ago.

Me-Larr turned to the other members of the Ruling Pack. "Spread the word to all the villages that we must go to arms. For many seasons we have lived for fighting. Now we must fight to live." He held the sword aloft. "Our foes will fall before us!"

All the Ruling Pack—save for Me-Larr and Te-Run—howled their approval. The sound pierced the air, and they howled in such perfect harmony that the metals in Klag's uniform seemed to vibrate.

Then the dozen members of the Pack who had

howled departed to carry out Me-Larr's instructions, leaving Klag alone with Me-Larr and Te-Run.

After a moment of silence, Te-Run spoke softly. "I knew that this day would come, but never did I believe it would come so soon—nor that it would come from your people, Captain Klag."

"Neither did I, Te-Run," Klag said honestly. "In truth, I am still amazed that this is happening. I have watched the message that Talak sent me informing me of his intentions many times, yet I cannot believe that it is a Klingon general speaking. I had thought the days of such honorless, cowardly behavior to be behind us as a people."

Me-Larr put his sword back on the wall. "You were obviously mistaken."

"Yes. With your permission, Me-Larr, I will begin transporting troops to the surface. They will begin instructing your own warriors in how best to combat our ground troops."

Baring his teeth, Me-Larr said, "That won't be necessary. If you recall, we had little trouble dealing with your ground troops when they first arrived."

Klag scowled. "This time it will be different. Talak is likely to send more than a hundred troops in the initial attack, and he is also aware of your capabilities."

"How is that?" Te-Run asked sharply. "You said you would share no intelligence with the enemy."

"Talak has our initial reports. I sent him records of our encounters to date when I first informed him of this planet, shortly after the final contest. I did not know then what his reaction would be. He *is* my commanding officer. Until I received his own obscene orders, I had no reason to mistrust him. So he knows of your capabilities, your passion, your fire. That gives him an advantage that the *Gorkon* soldiers did not have a week ago. So we must give you a further advantage."

"Very well." Me-Larr seemed very reluctant to concede the point, for which Klag couldn't really blame him.

"Worry not, Me-Larr—I will not allow your world to be taken from you without a fight."

Me-Larr nodded. "I *do* worry, Captain Klag—but not about that. I am responsible for my people, and I fear that I may have led them into ruin."

"You've done no such thing," Te-Run said snappishly. "If anything, you've given us the best hope we have for survival. Imagine if General Talak had come instead of Captain Klag here. He would not have accepted our challenge, and they quite likely would have destroyed us all. Now we have an ally in our fight, and one who knows the foe better than we do." She cradled Me-Larr's snout in one claw. "Either way, Me-Larr, you are leading us to the greatest battle the Children of San-Tarah have ever seen. Win or lose, you have guaranteed that yours will be the story most told by future generations."

Me-Larr did not sound convinced. "And if we are wiped out?"

"Then you will be at the forefront of those who run with the dead."

Klag assumed that this was a good thing. It didn't cheer Me-Larr as much as Klag thought it should, however, so the captain added, "Te-Run is wise, Me-Larr. I have learned in my time as captain of the *Gorkon* that it is better to listen to wise counsel than to ignore it."

"You are both, of course, correct." He bared his teeth. "It will be our most magnificent fight."

Smiling, Klag activated his communicator. "Klag to *Gorkon*."

His first officer replied, "*Kornan*."

"Have *QaS DevwI'* Vok, Klaris, and B'Yrak transport down with their troops for training with the Children of San-Tarah."

"*Yes, sir.*"

That would put the two hundred and twenty-five best ground troops from the *Gorkon* on the surface. They would begin the work of training with the San-Tarah for the next five days until Talak's arrival. By the time the fleet did show up, Klag intended to have a thousand troops aiding the Children of San-Tarah. *You may win the day, General, but your victory will be the hardest-won of your misbegotten life.*

"*Bridge to Captain Triak.*"

Triak, son of H'Ren, captain of the *I.K.S. Kreltek*, looked up at the sound of his first officer's voice. Commander Vekma had been given strict orders not to disturb him. *Does that fool woman think that because we share a bed she may disregard my instructions?*

Before he could rebuke his second-in-command she added, *"I would not disturb you normally, Captain, but Lieutenant Hevna says she must see you immediately. That it is business of the highest order."*

"What kind of business?"

"She won't say," Vekma said, her voice dripping with anger. Triak smiled. Vekma did not like being uninformed. He suspected that her desire for him was as much due to the greater access she had to Triak and his thoughts as his bedmate than she would as simply his first officer. Since she was so adept at both, Triak did not mind. *"She will only say that it is urgent."*

Normally, Triak would tell Vekma that the first-shift pilot could either explain herself or not get her audience—and perhaps get rotated off the bridge—but Hevna was not given to this sort of thing, normally. She was one of his finest officers, and the best pilot he had ever served with; she performed Kalmat's Maneuver in battle against the Jem'Hadar during the war, which wasn't supposed to be possible with a ship as large as the *Kreltek*. She had even been inducted into the Order of the *Bat'leth* two months ago on Ty'Gokor.

"Very well. Send her in."

"As you wish." Vekma didn't sound happy. Triak suspected that she wanted the captain to refuse the request. *I may well pay for my accession tonight*, he thought with regret.

A moment later, the door to his tiny office rumbled open, and Lieutenant Hevna entered. Hevna was appallingly young—*or perhaps I'm simply getting old*, Triak thought with a bit of melancholy—with hardly any muscle on her whatsoever. Had he not known of her piloting prowess, he would not have thought to look at her that she was Defense Force material. But warriors fought their battles in their own ways with the weapons best suited to them, and Hevna's were the helm controls of spacefaring vessels.

"Speak, Lieutenant. And make it quick. I do not appreciate being disturbed."

"I know, sir, and I would not have done so were the reason not so important." She took a breath. "Captain, I must respectfully request that you divert the *Kreltek* to the Kavrot Sector for urgent business of the Order of the *Bat'leth*."

Triak stared incredulously at Hevna for a moment, then threw his head back and threw a hearty laugh at the ceiling. "Vekma put you up to this, did she not? I did not credit her with this vicious a sense of humor. Thank you, Lieutenant, you may—"

"Sir, this is not a joke. I have received a summons from a fellow member of the Order."

"And this is supposed to matter why, exactly?"

Hevna blinked. "Did Commander Vekma not tell you?"

"Tell me what?" This was rapidly turning less amusing and more irritating. If Hevna was not more forthcoming, she was going to taste his *d'k tahg*.

"Chancellor Martok has summoned the Order back to its original purpose."

"*What* original purpose?" Then a memory of the night after Hevna's induction came back to him, from his and Vekma's postcoital conversation, where she told him about the all-night celebrating followed by the induction ceremony. Triak had only been paying partial attention, as he had remained on the *Kreltek* for the whole thing—Vekma had always wanted to attend an Order induction, and Triak thought it would be imprudent for both captain and first officer to be off-ship for so long—and so had been denied Vekma's company the previous night. He was mostly eager to make up for lost time, so he had forgotten. "Wait, something about spreading the word of Kahless—?"

Hevna breathlessly explained to Triak what Martok had said regarding the Order. *So old Chancellor One-Eye wants to drag that foolishness from the past back to the present? This is what happens when commoners are given power.* He remembered now that he had laughed at Vekma when she had told him of it two months ago, and dismissed it as romantic foolishness.

"And now one of the inductees has decided to use this as an excuse to summon the Order?" he asked.

"Yes. Captain Klag has—"

"Klag?" Triak knew of Klag: the son of M'Raq, who, like some kind of human, used his father's right arm to replace the one he lost during the war. If they were letting animals like *Klag* into the Order, then its future as a means of maintaining honor in the Empire was a bleak one indeed.

"Yes, sir. Captain Klag has given his word to—"

Triak held up a hand. "Enough. This conversation has gone on far longer than I should have allowed it. The *Kreltek* is assigned to patrol the outer colonies. Unless I receive orders from Command that say otherwise, I will not divert from that assignment."

"Sir, you have discretion to—"

Angrily, Triak stood up, unsheathing his *d'k tahg.* "I *do* have discretion, yes, Lieutenant, but I *certainly* will not use it to chase honorless *jatyIn* conjured by a fool such as Klag! If you say one more word on this subject, you will be rotated off the bridge—assuming I do not decide to kill you." He held up his dagger, the outer blades clicking into their open position. "You have only lived this far into this discussion because of your accomplishments as a pilot. Am I understood, Lieutenant?"

Hevna stood at attention. "Yes, sir!"

"Good. Get out of my sight."

Without another word, Hevna turned on her heel and left the office.

Triak resheathed his weapon and sat back down. *Order of the* Bat'leth, he thought, shaking his head, *what a sad, pathetic joke.*

CHAPTER TWO

Upon his return to the *Gorkon*, Klag's first stop was the bridge. The Chancellor-class ship had a good-sized command center, with the captain's chair, of course, as its frontispiece. All Klingon vessels were designed with the bridge at the fore of the ship and the command chair at the fore of the bridge. After all, if captains did not literally lead warriors into battle, then they were not worthy of the honor of their position. It was also a symbol of trust: captains must be willing to leave their backs exposed to the crew.

To the captain's immediate right was the first officer's position, with the pilot to the left. Operations and weapons were right behind him, with secondary systems at various consoles aft.

Upon his entry, Klag went to the operations console. He was joined by Commander Kornan, who got up from the first officer's position, and Lieutenant

Toq, who had been laboring over that console when Klag entered.

"Captain," Kornan said, "Lieutenant Toq has good news."

"Such news would be welcome. Speak, Lieutenant."

The young lieutenant spoke with his usual youthful enthusiasm. "I believe I have found a way to fire torpedoes."

Klag's face broke into a grin. "That *is* good news." The subspace eddies had disrupted all weapons functions aboard the *Gorkon*, reducing the mighty vessel to a glorified troop transport, which did not sit well with its captain.

Toq returned a smile of his own. The eager young man had proven himself to be a fine officer in his months of service aboard the *Gorkon*, from his quick and brilliant technical solutions to his prowess in the hunt, which won the *Gorkon* their first contest against the Children of San-Tarah. "It will require attaching small shield generators to all of the torpedo casings, but I have found a shield modulation that will keep the photon torpedoes from becoming inert from the subspace interference."

"What of the quantum torpedoes?"

That eliminated Toq's smile. "The shields do not protect those torpedoes from the interference—they are still inert."

"And disruptors?"

"Still nonfunctional. I am, however, continuing to seek a solution."

Klag put an encouraging hand on the young lieutenant's shoulder. "Good. What of the subspace eddies?"

"Leskit and I are in the process of mapping them. I have also informed Commander Kurak that we may lose several key systems at inopportune moments if we slip into the eddies—but it will be as nothing compared with the fleet's difficulties. We will have had five days to verify these readings as well."

"Good." Klag turned to Kornan. "Run three simulations per day until the fleet engages us, with both pilots."

"Yes, sir," the commander replied.

"Leskit," Klag said to the old pilot, "I want you and Ensign Koxx to both be fully prepared for *any* maneuver you may have to make that will keep my ship intact, is that understood?"

"Completely, Captain." Leskit nodded his affirmation with sufficient enthusiasm to make his necklace of Cardassian neckbones rattle.

"Good." He looked around the bridge. "Continue your work. I want as many weapons as possible to function by the time the fleet arrives."

"We will, sir." Kornan spoke the words with confidence.

Klag regarded his first officer with something approaching respect. Kornan had spent his ten weeks as the *Gorkon*'s second-in-command filling the role, but doing little else. Klag had gone from Drex, the son of Martok and an incompetent fool who let his father's honor speak for him far too often, to Tereth, one of the best officers he'd ever served with, to Kornan during his time captaining this vessel, and this last man was the biggest enigma. Competent, certainly, but he never took initiative, never did more than was absolutely necessary to function. Unlike, say, Kurak—the chief engineer who had no desire to excel—Kornan did not choose to be this way, it simply seemed all he was capable of.

However, since Klag had shown him General Talak's message, it was as if someone had lit a fire under the commander. *Let us hope it lasts.*

"I will be in the medical bay."

Klag departed the bridge through the rear exit, his substitute bodyguard falling into step behind him. The captain wanted his best soldiers on the surface, so his usual bodyguard—Morr, the Leader of First Squad—was on the planet. Part of him wasn't concerned. He doubted that any of the senior officers had designs on his position. On the other hand, he *was* ordering them to go into battle against their fellow Klingons. This was not a situation to be taken lightly, and not one that all Klingons would approve of. He made a mental note to speak to Lieutenant Lokor, the chief of ship's security, about possibly doubling his guard.

He arrived at the medical bay to see only two occupants: Dr. B'Oraq and Lieutenant Rodek. All the others who had been injured during the contests with the Children of San-Tarah had apparently been discharged. *Good,* Klag thought. *It is not fit for warriors to lie in bed waiting for their bones to mend.*

Rodek, however, had sustained great injuries during the marine combat and was still unconscious.

Or, rather, he had been, Klag amended as he saw that Rodek's eyes were finally open.

"Captain," B'Oraq said. "I was just going to contact you. As you can see, I have good news." The doctor moved as if to tug on the auburn braid that hung over her right shoulder, secured by a pin in the shape of the emblem of her House, but she stopped short of doing so. Klag smiled.

"It is good that you are conscious, Lieutenant."

"Thank you, sir," the gunner said, sounding remarkably sharp-witted for someone who had just awakened from a several-day coma.

Turning to the doctor, Klag asked, "How soon can he be returned to duty?" The *Gorkon's* other primary gunner, Morketh, was killed in the same engagement that injured Rodek. Although their substitutes were adequate in general, Klag preferred to have a more experienced hand on deck for the coming battle.

"I am ready to return now, sir," Rodek said before B'Oraq could speak.

"No, you really aren't," B'Oraq said quickly, and turned to the captain. "Sir, I don't even think he should be getting out of the biobed for another day. Half his chest was blown apart, and the head injury was quite severe."

Rodek sat up. Klag noted that there was a bandage

on the right side of his head. "I am ready to return to duty, sir. I would ask that I be allowed to take my station."

"I won't authorize that," B'Oraq started, but the gunner interrupted her.

"This is not a human ship, Doctor—you have no authority to—"

"But I do, Rodek," Klag said firmly. "And if B'Oraq will not authorize your return to duty, then I will not override her."

"Sir, I have come up with a possible way to do battle within the field of subspace eddies. I wish to test the theory. I realize that Morketh or one of the other gunners may do so, but I wish—"

"Morketh is dead, Lieutenant," Klag said. "And we are about to *do* battle in the field." Quickly, Klag filled the gunner in on the current situation.

"In that case, Captain, I *must* return to duty."

"If you return to duty, Lieutenant," B'Oraq said tightly, "you'll probably be dead in minutes. Certainly if you go into any kind of combat situation—"

"I am not some mewling child to be coddled back to health, woman!" Rodek barked.

That took B'Oraq aback. In truth, it did the same for Klag. Though Rodek was a fine warrior, he had always come across as passionless. This was the most animated Klag had ever seen him.

B'Oraq's surprise, however, was fleeting. "No, but you are only alive because of me, Lieutenant."

"You are the ship's doctor," Rodek said dismissively. "It is your duty to—"

Shaking her head, B'Oraq said, "You misunderstand—you are alive *because of me*. The *Gorkon* medical bay was designed to *my* specifications, and incorporates improvements and upgrades to the standard medical bay that *I* insisted upon. If it weren't for those upgrades, you would be with Morketh in *Sto-Vo-Kor* right now. You had a subdural hematoma and dozens of chest wounds. Believe me when I tell you that I know *precisely* how close you were to death, and how difficult your journey back will be. You are *not* fit for duty, and if you attempt to report for duty, I will not accept *any* responsibility for your health whatsoever." This last she said with a significant look at Klag.

The silence hung in the medical bay for only a moment. Then Klag spoke. "What is this plan you have, Lieutenant?"

With a glower at the doctor, Rodek lay back down. "It was something we did on the *Hegh'ta*. I thought of it while we were on that wind boat on the planet, but I did not have a chance to report my idea. We mine the eddies with modified torpedoes. If we add shield generators to the torpedoes, the interference won't neutralize them."

Klag threw his head back and laughed. "Toq is ahead of you, Rodek. He has already succeeded in modifiying the photon torpedoes so that we can fire them. For that reason, your plan is unworkable. We will require the photons for actual combat."

Rodek said nothing.

"Will your plan work with probes?" Klag asked after a moment's thought.

Blinking, Rodek turned his head to look up at the captain. "I believe so, yes."

"Good. True, we're supposed to use the probes for our exploratory mission, but those endeavors have been cut short." He turned to B'Oraq. "Doctor, Rodek will go on restricted duty. He will not take the gunner's position, but he will be available to supervise the implementation and testing of his plan. If we can mine the subspace eddies, it will give us a huge advantage."

Bracing himself for an argument, Klag was pleasantly surprised to hear B'Oraq say, "Very well." The doctor was as stubborn and argumentative as her captain, but annoyingly she was right all the time. That was why he had supported her refusal to let Rodek return to active duty—but his plan would be of far too much use to let him fester here.

"Report to Kornan on the bridge."

"Yes, *sir*." Gingerly, Rodek rose from the biobed, and then—without aid, which he did not ask for, nor did Klag or B'Oraq offer it—he exited the medical bay, walking slowly, but with a confidence that Klag had never seen there.

"It would seem that Rodek's injury may have done him more good than harm in the long run." When B'Oraq did not respond, Klag turned to her. The doctor seemed lost in thought. "B'Oraq?"

"Hm? Oh, I'm sorry, Captain, I was just thinking. Something about what Rodek said is bothering me."

"What?"

"I'm not sure." She tugged on her braid, then self-consciously put her hand down. Klag had pointed out that nervous habit of hers, and ever since then, she'd been overconscious of it. "Was there something else you wanted to see me about?"

"Yes. You were giving rudimentary first aid to the San-Tarah before the contest ended. You will beam down immediately and begin those endeavors again. We need to give them every possible advantage."

B'Oraq shook her head and chuckled.

"Something amuses you, Doctor?"

"The entire situation. Two years ago, if you'd told me that a Klingon captain would view first-aid training as a tactical advantage, I'd have said you were insane."

Klag smiled. "These last few months have taught me of the efficacy of being able to return whole warriors to the field of battle." The words were B'Oraq's own, chosen deliberately. Klag had been raised with the same disdain for medicine that most Klingon warriors had, viewing such treatment as a weakness. B'Oraq had shown him that it was, in fact, a strength, one which he himself had embodied by allowing her to fashion him with a new right arm.

"Thank you, Captain."

Nodding, Klag took his leave of the medical bay. There was still much to do before Talak—and who-

ever might have answered Klag's call to arms—
arrived.

H'Ta, son of Kahmar, turned the battered old viewer
off. The face of some captain named Klag faded from it.

He removed the Order of the *Bat'leth* medallion
from the viewer and stared at it. The light from the
late-day sun that shone through the window reflected off the tarnished metal. The medallion had
sat in a trunk for years. H'Ta had not even thought
about the Order since shortly after his induction. Indeed, he remembered his induction as clearly as he
did only because the ceremony was interrupted by an
attack, which eventually revealed that the man
everyone believed to be General Martok was in fact
a changeling infiltrator from the Dominion.

H'Ta returned to duty after that. Later on, the real
Martok was restored to the Empire, and now he ruled
it as chancellor. But that was of little concern to
H'Ta, for Martok's triumphant return to his people
happened at about the same time that H'Ta had lost
his leg in battle against the Jem'Hadar.

Placing the medallion in the pocket of his one-
piece outfit, H'Ta grabbed the metal pole that leaned
against the wall of the small room and braced himself
against it in order to get up. Then he hobbled over to
the doorway to his sitting room and into the bed-
room. They were two of only four rooms in the
house, the others being the bathroom and the
kitchen. H'Ta didn't need much, after all.

Using the pole as a substitute leg, he worked his way back to the trunk. When he had come home from the day's work, the trunk had been beeping. It had taken him several minutes to locate the source: the Order medallion, buried under all his other Defense Force accoutrements.

H'Ta wasn't even sure why he kept them all. His *d'k tahg*, his armor, his medals—all had tarnished with lack of care over the last three years. There was no good reason to keep them, and every reason to throw them out.

He didn't care what new purpose the Order of the *Bat'leth* had been put to by Martok. As far as H'Ta was concerned, his membership in that august body ended when the Jem'Hadar blew his leg off. H'Ta had killed the Dominion soldier for that action, but his career ended then. A warrior could not go into battle with only one leg.

So he returned home to Galtran. Kahmar, H'Ta's father, was a farmer, as was his father before him. The House of Varrin, of which they were respected members, owned most of the farms on Galtran, providing nourishment for the people. For a long time, H'Ta was ashamed of his family's work. Songs were sung about farmers, but they were halfhearted, insincere paeans to those who fed the warriors who fought for the Empire. As the third son, he had no obligations to the family, and so was free to pursue a career in the Defense Force. In fact, his family encouraged it—his exploits in battle could only aid the family honor, and indeed his induction into the Order achieved that as well.

But then came the endless battles, the blood, the hardship, and the viciousness of the foes. H'Ta did not shy from battle, but he did grow weary of it. By the time the Jem'Hadar took his leg, he was ready to end it all, but saw no way to do so without sacrificing his honor, and that of his family.

Now, though, he had put the carnage behind him. He worked on the family farm, bringing sustenance to the Empire. H'Ta was content to let those more suited to battle have songs composed about them. He had his small house, his duties in the fields— mostly involving navigation of a plow, easily accomplished by a one-legged person—and the satisfaction of his work.

H'Ta, son of Kahmar, had no more use for battle. Let Captain Klag wade in blood. H'Ta preferred fertilizer.

CHAPTER THREE

Klag entered the bridge at a dead run after he received Kornan's summons, his bodyguard hard-pressed to keep up with him. "Report!" he barked upon his entrance, before the aft doors could fully open.

"Five ships are entering the system," Kornan said from the first officer's position. He looked up at Klag. "They are *not* Talak's fleet."

"Are you sure?"

"Yes, sir—one is a *Vakk*-class ship. There is no such vessel assigned to Talak."

Klag's heart sang. If it wasn't Talak then it *had* to be the Order. *Five ships. We may win the day yet.* Plus, he knew he had a few more allies coming....

He turned to Toq. "Identify them—quickly!"

Toq was, of course, already working his console. "Computer is confirming identity beacons now, sir."

He looked up. "There is a *K'Vort*-class ship, the *I.K.S. Taj*."

That made Klag's heart sing anew. Commander T'vis of the *Taj* was a past inductee into the Order, and the ship's captain, B'Edra, was an admirer of Klag's. They had met at Klag's induction ten weeks earlier, and he had been hoping that she would rally to his side—and not only because she commanded so powerful a ship.

Toq read from his console. "Two are *B'Rel*-class birds-of-prey—the *I.K.S. Slivin* and the *I.K.S. Qovin*. The *Vakk*-class cruiser is the *I.K.S. Vidd*. And the last is a *Birok*-class strike ship." He looked up and smiled. "The *I.K.S. Ch'marq*."

"That is Grakal's ship, is it not?"

"Yes, sir," Toq said, still smiling.

"Who is Grakal?" Kornan asked.

"One of my fellow inductees," Klag said. "I had hoped he would respond." Still, he was not as heartened as he might have been. Birds-of-prey and strike ships had their place in battle, but as support. The *Vidd* and the *Taj* would be of use, but only the *Gorkon* itself had enough firepower to seriously challenge the general's own *Vor'cha*-class cruiser. And the general also had three of the *Karas*-class strike ships, which were more powerful than the older *Birok* class.

Of course, our firepower will be superior to all of them because we will have some within the subspace eddies, he thought. "What of the modifications?"

Kornan said, "Lieutenant Rodek is in engineering,

aiding Commander Kurak in the modifications to the probes. The commander wishes to lodge a complaint about the unnecessary tampering with her equipment."

"Of course she does," Klag snarled. Kurak's truculence was not improving with time as he'd hoped. *It would seem I will have to address that.* He had hoped that Kurak would adjust her attitude in a favorable direction, but she had, if anything, grown worse. "How soon will they be ready?"

"Their last report indicated that most of the probes would be done by the end of the shift."

"I want them *all* done by the end of the shift. Have her bring in additional personnel if necessary."

"Yes, sir."

Klag turned to Toq. "Have the eddies been fully mapped yet?"

Toq nodded. "Leskit has plotted several courses for navigation through the eddies." Then he smiled. "I'm afraid any plans you have to kill him will have to wait—I believe he is the only person on the ship who can handle the maneuvering properly."

Klag grinned. "Pity, that."

"It's all part of my cunning plan," Leskit drawled from the pilot's station. "I'm trying to make myself indispensable."

"Some of us would settle for useful," Klag said, then dropped the grin. "Prepare the full navigational data. I wish to inspect it." He walked toward his chair. "Contact the approaching ships, Toq. I would speak with our potential allies."

Kornan followed him toward the fore of the bridge. "Potential?"

"We are asking a great deal, Commander. I do not know all these captains—and some of them are responding to a call made to members of their crew. For example, I know that the *Taj* is here because of its first officer, not Captain B'Edra. I wish to speak to them, know their minds, their hearts, before I will trust them enough to call them allies." Slowly—after over half a year as captain, he had yet to grow tired of savoring this particular action—Klag sat in the command chair.

Kornan took his seat at the first officer's position to his right. "Understandable, Captain."

"The ships are responding, Captain," Toq said. "The commander of the *Vidd* claims to speak for the convoy—Captain K'Vada wishes to speak to you."

Interesting, Klag thought. *They have already convened a discussion—probably when they encountered each other growing closer to the star system. That explains why they came in on the same vector. They picked each other up on long-range and met.* He wasn't sure if that was a good sign or not, but chose to be cautiously optimistic. "Activate screen."

The image of San-Tarah on the main viewer was replaced with that of a sour-faced man with a fairly simple crest. "*Greetings, Captain Klag. I am K'Vada, and I wish to thank you.*"

"For what?" Klag asked cautiously.

"For one thing, your summons enabled me to solve a personnel problem. For another . . ." K'Vada's face broke into a smile that made the captain look like a predator about to consume its prey. *"My Order medallion was buried in a drawer, long since forgotten. I am grateful for the reminder of what it means to be a Klingon."*

"That is good to hear, Captain, because our worth as Klingons will be put to the test. All the ship captains will gather in the *Gorkon* wardroom in half an hour. We will form our strategy."

"I hope that includes a way to find the planet in question. We're barely able to detect it."

Klag smiled. "We can do far better than that, Captain. All will be revealed in half an hour. In the meantime, we will send you the sensor modifications we made in order to detect the planet."

"That will be appreciated. Half an hour, then."

"Screen off."

From behind him, Toq spoke. "Sir, we've received the latest dispatches from Command. Brenlek has officially been made part of the Klingon Empire. A planetary governor has been appointed—and General Talak is now proceeding to do the same for San-Tarah."

Normally, this news would be greeted with cheers—the bringing of another world under the heel of the Empire was often cause for rejoicing—but the bridge remained quiet.

Klag rose smoothly from his chair—without listing to the right, he realized after he did so—and said quietly: "It begins." He turned to Kornan. "I will be in the wardroom preparing for the meeting. Have Lokor escort our guests when they arrive."

"What you ask is impossible."

Kornan tried to control his reactions to Commander Kurak, made more difficult by how contradictory they were. The chief engineer both maddened and enthralled him. She was one of the most attractive women he'd ever met, yet he had done a poor job of ingratiating himself with her. Knowing ahead of time from reading the *Gorkon*'s records that Kurak's relationship with the ship's command structure had been a difficult one, Kornan had done everything he could to make their professional relationship smooth. To improve matters, he found her attractive, and she reciprocated the feeling—at least at first. But then there was the disastrous marine combat on San-Tarah, an engagement that Kurak—who numbered sailing on wind boats among her most passionate hobbies—led and on which Kornan had served as crew. Its poor outcome had led Kurak to excoriate Kornan and everyone else involved.

Her anger, her fire, her fury only served to make her more attractive to him.

This fond desire, however, warred with an equally fond desire to have her killed for her insolence. He was still her superior officer, after all. They stood now on the outskirts of the engineering section, the rest of the staff giving them both a wide berth—or, perhaps, simply avoiding Kurak herself. From what

Lokor, the security chief, had reported, discipline in engineering had remained balanced as any petty squabbles were superseded by a fear of Kurak's wrath combined with a healthy respect for the fact that nobody wanted her job.

"Make it possible."

Kurak barked a derisive laugh. "Were I capable of altering the laws of physics, then, perhaps, I could get the work done sooner, but if I could do that, we would have won our combat mission at sea." She glared at Kornan as she said that.

"If you need more staff, you may—"

"I have already conscripted both engineering shifts working double time. No one else on the *Gorkon* has the training, and the time it would take to instruct them would be longer than the time that would be saved by the extra pairs of hands." Kurak gripped her left wrist with her right hand. "On the bridge, you deal with honor and glory and duty—vague concepts that can neither be quantified nor controlled. Here, I deal with mechanical reality. It is unyielding, it is unbending, and no amount of screaming from you or the captain will change that. So tell Klag that he will have approximately seventy percent of the probes modified by the end of the shift, with the rest done as soon as possible after that. If that does not satisfy him, then he can have me killed and replace me as chief engineer." Kurak smiled most unpleasantly. "However, should he do so, I can guarantee that the percentage of completed probes will be much less than seventy. Which will also be the case if you don't stop pestering me!"

Kornan didn't think it was possible to be this aroused and this furious at the same time. They stood, face-to-face, for a long moment. He smelled the *raktajino* on her breath, mixing with the other scents of her body, and had to fight down simultaneous urges to rip her uniform off and to run her through with his *d'k tahg*.

He finally spoke. "I will convey your words to the captain—*all* of them."

"Good. If there isn't anything else, *Commander?*" She almost sneered the rank.

"Yes. The captain also wishes you to find a way to make the disruptors function amidst the subspace eddies. His exact words were: 'Kurak claims to be the finest engineer in the fleet. I should think this task would be within her capabilities.' "

Kurak snorted. "Yes, if I had a proper research team and several months to test possible retunings of the disruptors, then I *might*—"

"This is not the Science Institute, Kurak!" Kornan bellowed. "This is the Defense Force. I have been willing to accommodate your eccentricities in light of your brilliance, but I begin to see now why all the reports filed by Klag, Drex, and Tereth on your performance of duty read like they did. You *will* perform your duties as chief engineer of this ship, is that understood, *Commander?*"

"Of course, *sir.*" Kurak then turned on her heel

and went to one of the consoles. The *bekk*s staffing that particular station scattered like *glob* flies in the presence of a *grishnar* cat's tail.

Advancing toward a turbolift, Kornan tried to figure out how to construct his report to the captain. In his two and a half months serving as Klag's first officer, he had come to see how the *Gorkon*'s commander had gained his peculiar reputation. When Kornan had been told of his assignment as the vessel's first officer, the first thing he had done was inquire about the man he'd be serving under. He found no shortage of opinions. But for every ten warriors he queried about Klag, he received twelve different answers. He was, at once, the bravest captain in the fleet and the most cowardly, the mightiest warrior and the weakest, honorable, fair, dishonorable, treacherous, brutal, merciful, merciless, inspirational, divisive. In his time on board, Kornan had found that, in his own estimation, the positive impressions were more prevalent than the negatives, but he could also see how Klag had come by so odd a legacy. He was like a flag atop its pole: yielding when necessary, but always rooted with a solid base.

Kornan knew that he was unworthy of serving with such a captain. He had thought himself ready for the responsibilities of second-in-command of a warship, but the past ten weeks had proven that to be a fallacious assumption. Years of serving on the *Rotarran* under a collection of underachieving, honorless *petaQ* in command only served to highlight Kornan's own inadequacies in the same position now. He did not stand for the crew, he did not serve his captain. At best, he held his ground, not advancing enough to conquer, though defending sufficiently not to retreat.

He was adequate.

What a horrid epitaph for a warrior.

As he entered the turbolift and instructed it to take him to the bridge, Kornan admitted something else to himself: This taking up of arms against General Talak would do nothing to change the gossip about Captain Klag, and might indeed cement all the negative feelings and eliminate the positive. But deeds, not gossip, paved the way to *Sto-Vo-Kor,* and whether or not they won the day, Kornan knew in his heart that the *Gorkon* would serve the cause of honor no matter what.

And if I cannot be worthy of such a battle, at the very least I will prove myself not to be unworthy of it.

Sometimes, that was all one could hope for.

"You realize that what you propose is treason."

Klag had resigned himself to the fact that not all those who answered his summons would necessarily be pleased with his course of action, but he had at least maintained some hope that they would all be enthusiastic. What was even more disheartening was that the sentiment was expressed by Captain B'Edra. *Admittedly,* Klag thought, *it is not entirely unexpected. She is the only person in the room who has not been inducted into the Order.*

She, Klag, and the other commanders of the ships that had answered Klag's call were in the *Gorkon*'s wardroom. B'Edra had declined a seat, instead standing against a bulkhead near the entrance. Klag also stood, but at the other end of the table. Captain K'Vada and Commander Grakal sat on one side, with the two captains of the birds-of-prey—Ankara of the *Slivin* and Daqset of the *Qovin*—facing them on the other side. The last time Klag saw Grakal, he had been unconscious after the all-night drinking binge that preceded the induction ceremony—and even when they'd first met, Grakal had partaken quite liberally of the bloodwine. In sobriety, his eyes had a fire that Klag had not seen on Ty'Gokor, and an intelligence as well.

Klag paced the wardroom toward B'Edra. "In the literal sense of violating the orders of a superior, you are correct. But were the warriors who defended Gowron against those who had allied with the traitorous House of Duras committing treason?"

"Of course not, but this is hardly the same thing."

To Klag's joy, it was K'Vada who replied. "It is exactly the same thing. House Duras allied themselves covertly with the Romulans and splintered the High Council by trying to shove Duras's bastard in as a legitimate candidate for chancellor. General Talak now asks a Klingon to go back on his word given to an honorable foe. Perhaps not the same scale, but the principle is the same—it is a point of honor."

"Is it?" Daqset asked. He had removed his *d'k tahg* upon entering, though without unfurling the side blades, and was now twirling it absently in his hands. "These aliens are animals, nothing more. A word given to them is like a word given to a *targ.*"

"Have you met them?" Klag asked, whirling on the captain. "Have you fought them? I have. They are among the finest warriors I have ever encountered, and the most honorable foes that any Klingon could hope for. If you wish, I will have the recordings of some of our combat with them made available to you."

"All that proves is that you are weak, and cannot defeat creatures fit only to be *jeghpu'wI'.*"

Klag snarled. "Are you challenging me, Captain?"

Daqset smiled unpleasantly. "Not yet. But I do wish to see these recordings before committing my ship to your doomed quest."

Ankara rose from her chair. "I too would like to view the records, but I do not feel that the quest is doomed. If a Klingon cannot count on his word, then our entire way of life becomes meaningless. Some may be prepared to live with that. I am not." Unsheathing her own *d'k tahg,* Ankara unfurled the blade and then sliced through her own palm. "I swear my fealty to your crusade, Captain Klag."

K'Vada stood and did the same. "As do I."

Daqset remained seated.

Grakal—who had been surprisingly quiet, given how voluble he'd been at the induction ceremony— finally spoke. "I will fight as well. The Empire is meaningless without honor. How many times have we as a people turned our backs on Kahless? The only way we have been put back on the right path is for warriors such as Klag to take the lead—to remind us of who we are. The battle against the Children of San-Tarah has already been fought. We must move on to new challenges now—and we must make General Talak see that." He removed his dagger and sliced his palm.

As the blood of three warriors stained the deckplates of the wardroom floor, Klag turned to B'Edra and smiled. "Well, Captain? Will you join us in our treason?"

B'Edra's expression was distressingly unreadable. The *Taj*'s captain had a small, round face with a single-ridged crest and short, curly brown hair. Her black eyes were unusually large for so small a face, and it almost made her look helpless, until you saw the hard lines of her mouth.

Finally, she said, "I will not swear fealty to you, Captain, for I am not a member of the Order. I am only here because my first officer insisted that I hear you out. Having done so, I am convinced that your cause is just, and the *Taj* will be at your disposal in your conflict with General Talak."

Klag was relieved by this; leaving aside any other considerations, the *Taj* was by far the most powerful ship besides the *Gorkon* in his minuscule fleet. "Thank you, Captain—and thank you all. You will not regret this." He pressed a control on his wrist, and the door opened to his bodyguard and another soldier. To the latter, he said, "Escort all but Captain

Daqset to the transporter room." Klag regarded Daqset. "Captain, you will remain here while I show you just what the Children of San-Tarah are capable of." Looking back at the other four, he added, "I will have all the information on the subspace eddies that we have compiled sent to your ships."

"Thank you, Captain," K'Vada said.

"And know this," Ankara added, "whether or not we live through what lies ahead, the victory is already ours."

Daqset laughed at that. "You are all fools. I will view these records of yours, Captain Klag, and perhaps I will lend the *Qovin* to your fleet. But do not expect this to end in anything but a swift journey to *Sto-Vo-Kor*."

General Talak gazed out upon his fleet on the viewscreen of the bridge of his flagship, the *I.K.S. Akua*. A dozen ships orbited the new Klingon planet of Brenlek, plus the *K'mpec*.

Now it was time to move on to San-Tarah.

Talak's concerns were far greater than the mere taking of a world. Klag's presence was an affront to Talak. For years, the filthy *toDSaH* had remained as first officer of the *Pagh*, preferring to bask in the reflected glory of Talak's Housemate, Captain Kargan, than to forge his own path of honor. Then, when Kargan died nobly at Marcan V during the Dominion War, Klag took all the credit. "The Hero of Marcan V," they called him.

It made Talak ill. Why this *petaQ* was given a

Chancellor-class ship to command—not to mention induction into the Order of the *Bat'leth*—when so many worthier captains were out there was a source of great confusion to Talak. But Martok found Klag to be an honorable man, and Talak could not afford to defy Martok's wishes. The one-eyed chancellor was just the person the Empire needed to lead it into an honorable future, one not laden with the petty corruptions and political compromises of regimes past.

Instead, Talak had waited until Klag did something to dishonor himself—an inevitability, truly— and he had done so. *A word given to* jeghpu'wI' *is no word at all*, he thought. *Let him have all the contests he wishes—it means nothing. San-Tarah will be part of the Empire, and Klag will be shown for the fool that I have always known him to be.* Klag's first officer was a man who had served with Martok on the *Rotarran* during the war, and Talak was sure, once Talak's *tik'leth* blade found Klag's heart, that Kornan would make a much more worthy captain of the *Gorkon*.

Unless, of course, Klag defies me, in which case, I will destroy him and his crew and leave them all in the disgrace they so deserve. Let them all ride the Barge of the Dead. Serving under Klag, they're halfway there already.

Aiding him would be Klag's own brother, Dorrek. The *K'mpec*'s captain had his own reasons for hating his sibling—something about their father—and Talak was more than happy to take advantage of that for his own ends. The House of K'Tal had suffered at

Klag's hands, and if Talak could be instrumental in destroying Klag while ingratiating himself with the person who would be the new head of Klag's House, it would only serve him well.

"Incoming transmission from Captain Huss, sir," said the voice of the operations officer from behind Talak.

The general frowned. Huss commanded three birds-of-prey, *Nukmay, Khich,* and *Jor.* Their atmospheric strikes had been instrumental in neutralizing the ground-based defenses that the natives of Brenlek had brought to bear on Talak's ground troops and on the ships in orbit. "Put it on the viewer."

"She wishes to speak in private, sir."

Whirling around, Talak regarded the operations officer and squinted his gray eyes at her. "Does she?"

Quickly, the officer said, "I am merely repeating her words, General."

He rose from his chair. "Very well. Inform her that I will take the communication in my office, and I will see what it is that compels such audacity from a captain to a general."

"Yes, sir."

Talak entered his office slowly, seeing no reason to rush to satisfy Huss's need for privacy. She was a fine captain, it was true, and her three ships had served well as part of Talak's armada during the war. But requesting a private audience in such a manner was not something he would reward—at least, until he knew its purpose.

After inspecting the contents of his office—he had decorated the space with several examples of his family's weaponry, including a three-hundred-year-old *gIntaq* spear and a fifty-year-old *d'k tahg* that his House Head, K'Tal, had worn when he first served on the High Council under the reign of Chancellor Ditagh—he finally activated the small viewer at his workstation. Captain Huss appeared on the screen. The captain had flame red hair that surrounded her long face like a glowing ember, and her oddly spotted crest had the complexity of a noble House indeed. She resembled Talak's favorite daughter, which he suspected was why he had invited Huss's fleet into his armada in the first place years ago, though she had, through her deeds, more than justified her placement.

"Speak."

"General, why am I being left behind?"

Eyes narrowing, Talak said, "You are remaining at Brenlek to provide support for Governor Worvag's installation." Worvag was the captain of the other three birds-of-prey in the conquering armada, and had earned the promotion after many years' long service. Talak would probably have offered it to Huss, but she had few ambitions beyond her current position, and was better suited to the life of a fleet captain than a politician. "We will return for you once San-Tarah is taken. I would have thought you'd be pleased by the honor."

"I believe that Worvag's former crew would be better to support him than I. They are suited to the tactical

nature of the assignment. My specialty is surgical strikes. Based on what we know of San-Tarah, you will need someone with our maneuvering skill."

Talak considered. He had thought Huss would prefer the honor of finishing the job at Brenlek, in case he had misread the situation and she *had* wanted the governor's position, plus he thought it would be better for Worvag's erstwhile crew to prove themselves without their former commander hanging over their heads.

"Besides," she added, "I have worked with Captain Klag before, at Narendra III. I believe I am better suited to accompany you to San-Tarah."

That got Talak's attention. He recalled that several ships—among them Huss's fleet—were placed in the mental thrall of a mad dictator named Malkus months ago, and that Klag, with the aid of a Federation starship, had liberated them.

"Very well, Captain Huss. You pose compelling arguments. You will accompany us to San-Tarah."

Huss grinned, showing attractively uneven teeth. *"Thank you, sir. I promise to serve the Empire with glory on this mission."*

"Of that I am sure, Captain. We will be departing Brenlek in three hours."

"We will be ready. Out."

He then put through a secure communication to Dorrek on the *K'mpec* and informed the captain of his change in plan.

Dorrek's face soured. His small, beady eyes looked even beadier when he did so. *"Why the alteration?"*

"Huss is better suited to the style of battle we will likely have to engage in, especially with the subspace eddies Klag spoke of. And she has an added benefit to *our* goals." He explained the Narendra III connection. "She has faced Klag in battle, even if she was under someone else's control when it happened. We can use that."

Then Dorrek grinned, but for some reason Talak found this captain's grin to be as repulsive as he found Huss's to be pleasant. "*Indeed we can. Thank you, General. Soon I will be able to wreak my revenge on my brother, and finally salvage our family's honor!*"

"Yes, you shall," Talak said patiently. "We depart in three hours. Be prepared."

CHAPTER FOUR

Leader Wol of Fifteenth Squad stood for just a moment, enjoying the feel of the breeze through her auburn hair, the warmth of the suns on her face, the scent of the animals and the flowers in her nostrils. Her previous two trips to the surface of San-Tarah involved combat, and she had been focused primarily on her duties then. This time, however, as they came down to help prepare for the ground troop invasion by General Talak and his dishonorable forces, she was able to spare a moment to enjoy the purity of this planet.

After spending so long in the regulated atmosphere of a ship, this is almost a relief. She had not been able to truly enjoy a natural setting such as this since her times spent hunting on the lands owned by the House of Varnak. *But that was another life.* Since being disgraced and exiled from that once-noble House, she had changed her name, joined the Defense Force as a common soldier, and spent all her time on bases and ships, her only excursions to the surface of a planet spent fighting for her life—and for her Empire.

It paid handsomely in the end, though, she thought with a bittersweet smile as she tasted the scent of a wild bird soaring overhead, and she longed for a spear to see if she could take it down and rend its head from its body and prepare it for a meal. *Varnak was disgraced when they aided in the coup against Chancellor Martok. And now I am a Leader of a favored squadron on a great ship serving under the finest captain in the fleet.*

"Leader."

Wol turned to see G'joth approaching her, Trant and Maris behind him. She had been sorry to lose Krevor—a bit less sorry to lose Davok, though he was a fine warrior when he needed to be—but at least now she had the opportunity to properly fulfill the responsibility that Lieutenant Toq had laid upon her shoulders. Trant and Maris would become proper warriors or die in the attempt.

"What do you want, G'joth?"

"I have a thought for a weapon we might be able to employ—one the general's forces will not be expecting. Are you familiar with a human weapon called a *mol'tov qaghteyl?*"

Frowning, Wol thought the second word sounded familiar, then placed it as a human word that usually applied to a beverage. "No," she said honestly, wondering where G'joth was going with this.

"Ambassador Worf used them on Narendra III. It involves placing a cloth of some kind in the neck of a bottle of alcohol, setting the rag alight, and then throwing the bottle."

"A fire bomb?"

G'joth nodded. "Exactly."

"Why not just start a fire?" Trant asked snidely.

Before Wol could respond, Maris did. "This enables you to do so from a distance and sow confusion among the enemy, allowing you to attack. And a spreading fire can be a great aid in battle."

"And a detriment," Trant added. "I think this is foolish."

The Leader spoke up. "Your thoughts are noted and discarded, *Bekk*."

"Something else," G'joth said

Wol had to keep from grinning at the *bekk*'s enthusiasm. *He hasn't been this excited since he first got the idea for writing an opera.* "Yes?"

"I believe that we can make other explosives. Some of the caves in the hills have mineral deposits that might be useful. But I'll need to talk to the ship to confirm the readings. If I'm right, we will have the makings of chemical explosives, which will be even more useful."

This made Wol growl with glee. "And won't be affected by the subspace interference."

"Exactly." G'joth grinned. "We should be able to construct some grenades."

Trant snarled again. "*Primitive* grenades, perhaps."

At that, Wol laughed. "How sophisticated does a grenade truly need to be, Trant?"

The *bekk* had no answer for that. Wol didn't really expect him to. Instead, he asked, "Am I the only one who finds this entire endeavor foolish? We are taking up arms against *Klingons*. General Talak ordered the captain to conquer this world. Should we not be doing so?"

G'joth regarded Trant as if he had grown another head. "The captain gave his *word*, Trant. In *my* universe, that *means* something to a Klingon. If it does not, perhaps you should not be wearing that uniform."

"I am more worthy to wear my uniform than an old fool like you, G'joth."

Wol stepped between them. "You have already been demoted once, Trant. I do not wish to see it happen again."

Gritting his teeth, Trant said, "I only wish to obey my orders!"

"Your orders were given to you by Captain Klag."

"*His* orders—"

"Are between him and General Talak. Our duty is to follow our commander."

G'joth added, "And I would much sooner follow Klag than some *petaQ* of a general who does not know the meaning of honor."

Maris finally spoke. "Trant has a point, loath as I am to credit him for it." Trant snarled at that, but Maris ignored him. "Our duty is to follow the orders of our superiors. If Captain Klag has failed in his duty, is it not ours to see that he is replaced with one who will?"

"Who, Kornan?" G'joth asked. "He supports the captain—as should we."

The *bekk*'s words served to forcibly remind Wol of her own past. Of the lowborn lover she chose to be with against the wishes of her noble House. Of her subsequent exile into the life of a Houseless woman. Of her years spent clawing her way through the Defense Force soldier ranks, where once she would have been accepted as an officer with no question.

And of her complete lack of regret. She had chosen her path, and had she the opportunity to do it again, she would do nothing differently.

"Sometimes, *Bekk*," she said to Maris, "one must choose between what is right and what is proper. Yes, it would be proper to blindingly obey the orders of our superiors. But what kind of Klingons would we be, then? I would rather die with honor than live with knowing that I had done wrong by the noble warriors of this planet." Turning to G'joth, she said, "Excellent work, G'joth. I will convey your suggestion to *QaS DevwI'* Vok."

With that, she suited action to words and walked to where Vok, first among the *Gorkon*'s troop commanders and Wol's commander, stood. The portly, brown-haired man was speaking with one of the Children of San-Tarah, a male with dark brown fur, whom Wol recognized as Ga-Tror, their Ruling Pack's Fight Leader.

Upon Wol's approach, Vok smiled broadly, his hands resting on his ample belly. "You have something to report, Leader Wol?"

"Yes, sir, I do." She outlined G'joth's proposal. "Permission to contact the ship so *Bekk* G'joth can verify the readings."

Ga-Tror spoke, then. "I thought your—tools did not work on our world?"

"Our small hand scanners do not," Vok said, "but the *Gorkon* sensors are powerful enough to cut through the interference."

"If you say so." Ga-Tror did not seem to understand, but since the Children of San-Tarah had no technology as such, he was unlikely to any time soon. "What I do not understand is why Captain Klag does not simply slay this one who behaves so dishonorably. Challenge him to fight in the circle."

If only it were that simple, Wol thought.

"That would be best," Vok said, "but it will probably not be feasible. Talak and the captain will probably never actually face each other."

Ga-Tror's mouth seemed to hang open for a moment. "How is that possible? How can they fight if they do not encounter each other?"

Vok seemed to struggle, so Wol came to his rescue. "They will face each other in space." She pointed up. "Above the skies." Then she remembered the marine combat. "Similar to how your people fought ours on the sea."

"Ah, so the *Gorkon* is like a wind boat, and you fire weapons at each other from a distance?"

"Yes."

Ga-Tror looked away. "I do not understand, though—can Captain Klag not call out a challenge to Talak, or board his ship?"

"Possibly, but Talak may not accept it. And our ships are enclosed—we have to communicate through technology." Wol was starting to get a headache. *They may be great warriors, but suddenly it is as if I am speaking to a child.*

"I still do not understand. Why can't he just call out to General Talak?"

Vok laughed. "That would hardly work in a vacuum."

"A what?"

"In space, it's a vacuum." At the Fight Leader's blank look, Vok added, "No air."

Ga-Tror laughed at that. "Don't be absurd. How can there be no air? The air is the air."

Vok opened his mouth, then closed it. He looked helplessly at Wol. *How do you explain the vacuum of space to a species that has never left its homeworld?*

"You will have to trust us," Wol finally said. "Once you go above a certain level, the air grows thinner. Have you never climbed one of the mountains?"

"Some have."

"And they've had trouble breathing as they get higher up, yes?"

Ga-Tror seemed to be growing impatient. "What does this matter?"

Wol was having trouble with that one herself, but she wasn't the one who had started this conversation. "For the moment, it doesn't. But there may well come a time when you will find yourself traveling off San-Tarah. You should know what is out there."

Ga-Tror looked Wol in the eyes. "That will never happen. We have all we need on San-Tarah. What possible reason could we have to leave it?"

Angrily, Wol asked, "Do you truly think we are your last encounter with—with beings from another world?" She wondered if Klingons were this foolish before the Hur'q invaded Qo'noS, plundering the Homeworld and taking their sacred treasures. That invasion led to the Klingon Empire's eventual domination of the stars, for they swore they would never be so defeated again. "Open your eyes, Ga-Tror—we are the *first* you have met. Others will come. Stories of your prowess will spread, as will tales of your world's riches. Even if we are victorious and drive away Talak's forces, others will come someday. You must be ready for that, and to be ready, you must know what the universe is like outside your world."

The Fight Leader looked away. "Perhaps we must, but that is not my concern today, nor will it be tomorrow. I am the Fight Leader of the Ruling Pack, and my duty is to prepare our people to fight."

Vok laughed and slapped Ga-Tror on the back. "As is mine, Ga-Tror, as is mine. We will save the philosophy for our victory celebration!" Turning to Wol, the *QaS DevwI'* asked, "Is there anything else, Leader?"

"Not at the moment, sir."

"Then take your squad to the ridge and join the third and twelfth in their drills until G'joth's information comes back from the ship. And Leader?"

"Yes?"

Vok grinned. "Well done. We will win this battle yet!"

Worf, son of Mogh, stood in the center of the workout room at the Federation Embassy on Qo'noS and tried to clear his mind.

Though born on this world, Worf grew up in the Federation after his family was massacred at the outpost on Khitomer. Chief Sergey Rozhenko—an engineer aboard the *U.S.S. Intrepid,* the first ship to respond to Khitomer's distress call after the Romulan attack that claimed four thousand lives—and his wife, Helena Rozhenko, raised him on the farming world of Gault and later on Earth. When he was old enough, Worf applied to Starfleet Academy and became the first of his species to serve in that august body.

Slowly, he began the forms of the *mok'bara.* An ancient Klingon martial art, the *mok'bara* reduced combat to a series of forms that purified the mind and purged the spirit. However, his movements were awkward this morning, the forms sloppy.

Worf had looked forward to serving the Federation as his father had, and in repaying the debt he owed to Starfleet.

What he had not expected was paperwork.

The word was a misnomer. Like many human terms, it was imprecise and based on an outdated model. In times past, such tedium was recorded with ink on wood pulp called *paper* instead of electronically, but the term remained in the lexicon even with its original meaning long having grown obsolete.

When he reported to the *Aldrin* as an ensign a decade and a half ago, Worf soon wished that the concept were as obsolete as the term. It never ended: reports that had to be filled out, logs that had to be recorded, sensor data that had to be double-checked. He entered the Academy with dreams of glory and honor. He soon learned that the path to glory and honor was paved with an endless pile of padds.

With each increase in rank and responsibility, that pavement became thicker. When he was promoted to junior-grade lieutenant, he became a bridge officer on the newly commissioned *Galaxy*-class *Enterprise*. The honor of serving on the vessel that was crowned the Federation flagship was great; so was the amount of paperwork.

As he rose in the ranks—full lieutenant and security chief on the *Enterprise*, lieutenant commander and strategic operations officer on the space station Deep Space 9—that only increased. Eventually, he grew accustomed to it, accepted it as part of his duty. It wasn't as if there was a shortage of opportunities for glory and honor to go with the tedious elements, from the first contacts with entities like Q and threats like the Borg on the *Enterprise* to being at the forefront of the Dominion War on DS9.

However, after the war, the Federation Council had offered him the posting of ambassador to the Klingon Empire. It was a job uniquely suited to Worf—he had his feet in both worlds, was a citizen of each nation, and was a hero in both as well—and one that enabled him to carry on for a fallen loved one. K'Ehleyr, the first woman he ever loved and the mother of his son, had been in that position when she died, and Worf thought of no better tribute to the memory of that magnificent woman than to continue her work.

Worf had succeeded beyond anyone's expectations. He aided Martok in consolidating his power base after the war, solved a crisis on taD, served the Federation well during a variety of incidents, helped smooth relations between the Klingon Empire and the Tholian Assembly when a past atrocity of the latter against the former came to light, and received great accolades for his presentations on the face of the galaxy in the wake of the Dominion War during the recent conference on Khitomer. Along the way, he occasionally participated in battle—against the false Iconians during the gateways crisis and against the mind-controlled minions of Malkus on Narendra III—to name but two such instances.

None of which mitigated the sheer tonnage of paperwork that his ambassadorial role entailed.

The door chime rang. He growled, and bellowed, "Enter!"

The doors to the small, featureless room parted and Worf's chief aide, Giancarlo Wu, came in. Wu had been serving at the embassy for the past eight years, and had proven invaluable. His organizational skills, patience, and ability to work easily with Klingons had been the primary reasons why Worf had not run screaming from the ambassadorship months ago.

"I'm sorry for interrupting, sir, but your wall is beeping."

Worf frowned. "My wall?"

"I believe that the beep is emanating from your Order of the *Bat'leth* medallion, sir."

After being inducted at Ty'Gokor two months ago, Worf had placed his medallion on the wall of his office at the embassy. He liked having the reminder of the honor where he—and his staff—would see it regularly.

But if it is beeping . . .

Without another word, Worf left the workout room, Wu at his heels. Several people passed him in the hallways, and gave him an odd look—the ambassador rarely moved through the hallowed halls of the embassy in his white skintight *mok'bara* shirt and pants and bare feet—but if the signal was what Worf thought it was, he would soon be called to battle.

Martok, who had welcomed Worf into his House years ago, had discussed the return of the Order to its original purpose with Worf. The chancellor felt that part of his mandate as head of the High Council was to help bring the people back to the traditional values that made the Empire great without the detritus of corruption and petty bickering and politics that the Empire had acquired over the centuries. Considering Worf's own role in having the clone of Kahless installed as Emperor in order to lead the people on that very path, not to mention the aid he had given Martok when a coup was launched against him shortly after the war, he would hardly do other than agree with the chancellor's reasons. As ambassador, he also felt that the Federation would be better served by an ally that wasn't being regularly racked with internal strife.

However, he had to admit that he hadn't expected the call to arms to come so soon.

The beeping assaulted his ears as soon as the door to his office parted. He walked straight to the wall where the Order medallion hung along with his baldric, the medals he'd been given during his Starfleet career, and the pictures of Alexander and K'Ehleyr, his wedding photo with the late Jadzia Dax, and the image of the "Niners" baseball team that Captain Sisko had assembled for a game against the crew of the *U.S.S. T'Kumbra.* Removing the medallion, he placed it in the workstation on his desk.

"Will you be needing me for anything else, sir?" Wu asked.

Worf had momentarily forgotten that the aide was present. The ambassador almost smiled. Wu was subtly reminding Worf of his presence and allowing Worf to let him know whether or not this communiqué was for Wu's eyes. In his eight months as ambassador, Worf had found Wu to be honorable, trustworthy, and invaluable. Besides which, Wu, for all intents and purposes, kept Worf's life running. If he was about to be summoned on any kind of Order business, Wu would need to be aware of it.

"Stay a moment," was all he said as he activated his terminal and had it decode the transmission.

Worf was hardly surprised that it was Klag who was the first to take Martok's plea to heart. The *Gorkon* captain had proven to be a man of singular honor and purpose.

When Klag's message ended, Wu spoke. "If I may ask, sir—what do you know of General Talak?"

"Very little. Chancellor Martok seems to trust him. However, his actions in this matter are—disturbing. If a Klingon captain cannot give his word to an honorable foe, then of what use is he?"

"I would say not much, sir."

"So often have I seen this—Klingons abusing power for their own ends. Duras and his Romulan-loving family, Gowron and his ambitions, Koroth and the other clerics at Boreth—and now this." Worf stood, prepared to jump to action, then stopped himself. *And of what use am I?* he asked himself. *I am no longer a Starfleet officer with a warship at my beck and call.* He longed to be able to take the *Defiant* or the *Enterprise* into action to assist Klag, but those days were behind him.

Wu rubbed his chin. "Odd thing, this new purpose that the chancellor has given to the Order."

Frowning at his aide, Worf asked, "What do you mean?"

"Well, the Order doesn't actually answer to the High Council, does it?"

"No—it acts independently."

"Which means, of course, that the High Council is unaware of what it does—or why it does what it does."

Rarely did Worf allow himself to smile. Years of living among fragile humans had taught him to restrain his natural Klingon passions to the point where he hardly knew how to do aught else. His all-too-brief marriage to Jadzia had loosened him up some, and he smiled more now than he ever did in the past.

Wu's clever reminder caused him to do so now.

Other members of the Order could bring ships to San-Tarah to force Talak and his fleet back to the course of honor. Worf had something they did not: the ear of the chancellor.

"Contact the Great Hall. I wish to see Martok immediately."

Wu smiled. "Very good, sir."

CHAPTER FIVE

"**R**eport," Klag barked as he entered the bridge from the aft entrance.

Kornan rose from the first officer's position. "Long-range sensors have detected ten vessels approaching the star system."

Klag smiled as he approached the operations and tactical consoles situated behind his command chair. He turned to Leskit. "Position report."

The pilot turned and grinned, his horn-trimmed beard quivering with the expression. "We are holding station at sixty thousand *qell'qams* from the most outlying of the subspace eddies."

To Toq: "The fleet?"

"They have taken up positions within the eddies that *should* render them invisible to a standard sensor scan."

Klag hoped that Toq was correct. Captain Daqset

had reluctantly agreed to go along after viewing the record of battle, willing to accept that the Children of San-Tarah were honorable foes. He did not, however, swear fealty, which distressed Klag. Still, even with Daqset and the *Qovin*, they were presently outnumbered two to one. They needed every advantage they could get....

"Weapons?" he asked *Bekk* Grint. Though Rodek had proven invaluable in advising on the modifications of the probe, by the time the work was done, he was barely able to stand up. At B'Oraq's strong insistence, he returned to the medical bay to recuperate, though not until he was sure that the probes had been successfully modified into mines.

"Disruptors and quantum torpedoes remain offline, even at this distance from the eddies." Grint gave his report with the eagerness of youth.

Klag had expected no less, but had been hoping for more. *Again, Kurak disappoints me.* After a moment, he amended, *No, to disappoint me, I must first expect something of her. Something must be done about her. A pity I have come to this realization now, on the eve of battle—and even if we are victorious, we are many light-years from home and a suitable replacement.*

Grint continued. "Photon torpedoes are armed and ready. Modified probes are deployed and ready to explode as soon as the honorless cowards enter our minefield."

"Then we are ready." Klag approached his chair

and, savoring it as he always did, slowly took his seat. Kornan did the same next to him. "When will our foes arrive?"

"Twenty-five minutes, sir." Kornan checked his status board. "We are now receiving identification of the fleet: One *Vor'cha*-class battleship, three birds-of-prey, two *K'Vort*-class heavy cruisers, three *Karas*-class strike ships—" Kornan looked up at Klag. "—and one Chancellor-class warship."

Klag clenched the fist that once belonged to his father. "Dorrek. I should have expected Talak to bring him along."

"That matches General Talak's fleet, less three birds-of-prey—and the addition of your brother's ship, sir," Kornan added.

"No doubt the three ships were left behind to finish the job at Brenlek."

Kornan nodded. "Yes, sir."

Toq then said, "Sir, you are being hailed—by Captain Dorrek of the *K'mpec*."

Whirling around in his seat to face the second officer, Klag said, "*I* am being hailed?"

"Yes, sir."

What in Kahless's name does Dorrek have to say to me now? "I will take it in my office." He rose directly from the chair, and stumbled slightly to the right. No one said anything, and Klag managed not to react. "Commander," he said through gritted teeth to his first officer, "be sure we are at full battle readiness."

The last time Klag and Dorrek had encountered each other was on Ty'Gokor, shortly after the induction ceremony, when Chancellor Martok had given the two of them, and the other ten captains of Chancellor-class vessels, their assignment to conquer the Kavrot Sector. Then, the last words his younger brother spoke to him were, "there is blood between us, and it will not end until one of us is in *Gre'thor*."

So far we have fallen, Klag thought as he entered his office. Once, he and Dorrek were as inseparable as twins, though they were born a year apart. For all the years that they were eligible—from the ages of four to nine—they entered the *bat'leth* competitions for the young, and in the years they both entered, they always finished first and second.

Once, when Klag was seven and Dorrek six, their great-uncle, an old one-eyed razorbeast named Nakri, took them on a *targ* hunt. Their father was off serving in the Defense Force at the time. While trying and failing to scent a *targ*, Dorrek caught wind of a *klongat*. Such beasts were difficult to kill even for seasoned hunters.

"We should try to bring it down," Klag had said as soon as he, too, caught the scent.

"It smells very large, brother," Dorrek said. "And Nakri has forbidden us to hunt anything so large on our own."

Klag laughed. "We are not on our own, brother— we are together. We are the sons of M'Raq. Is there nothing we cannot do?"

At that, Dorrek smiled. "If there is, we have not yet encountered it."

"Exactly. I am sure that, if one of us did try to hunt the *klongat* on our own, that one would die. But we are together—we are strong."

"But Klag—"

Seeing that this brother was vacillating, Klag took the road that always worked, for as a boy, at least, Dorrek knew the meaning of honor. "I am the *older* brother, Dorrek. When Father is away, I lead our House. We *will* hunt this beast." Then he laughed again—a shadow of the heavy-throated laugh he would develop in his later years—and slammed Dorrek on the back. "Do not worry, brother—we shall subdue the creature with little difficulty."

Klag's hypothesis proved accurate to a point, if one considered "little difficulty" to include dozens of broken bones each, head trauma, the tip of one of Dorrek's fingers sliced off, and half of Klag's hair ripped out.

But the *klongat* fell.

Now, decades later, the rift caused by their father's refusal to reclaim his honor after his escape from the Romulans made such memories bittersweet. *My brother and I will never hunt again, unless it is to seek out the other and kill him.* Where Klag felt only contempt for Talak and his House, he felt pity for his brother. *He once knew the path of honor.*

He activated the viewscreen on his desk, and Dorrek's face—long where Klag's was angular, beady-eyed where Klag's eyes were wide and open—

appeared. *"Klag, this is foolish. Tell your fleet to stand down and let General Talak do his duty."*

Klag blinked. "What?"

"We know you called in the Order of the Bat'leth, Klag. Your surprise won't work. I assume you've got them hiding in that mess of subspace tears out there to ambush us."

Klag said nothing, though he was disappointed. *It had been a calculated risk. Such a wide-ranging call as mine meant there was a good chance that word of it would reach Talak's ears before their arrival.* "If you truly think me so cowardly as to surrender now—"

"Cowardly?" Dorrek laughed. *"No, brother, there are many words I would use to describe you, none of them favorable, but 'coward' is not among them. I am quite sure that you will go bravely to a fool's death. And believe me, you will die a fool. The Order's era is in the past, Klag. We are no longer feudal lords fighting over mountains with primitive bat'leths. We are soldiers of a great Empire, a sophisticated people who are beyond such outdated concerns."*

At that moment, Klag ceased pitying his brother.

"Is honor outdated? We fought the Dominion—I lost my arm—to preserve our way of life. I will not see it thrown away by shortsighted fools such as you and Talak."

"Our way of life?" The reasonable tone Dorrek had been using, no doubt in a misguided attempt to appeal to Klag's better nature, was gone, replaced with the anger Klag had seen on Ty'Gokor weeks ago. *"What do you know of a Klingon way of life, Klag? You,*

*who mount our father's arm to your shoulder like some
kind of sick trophy?"*

"Do not try to claim some kind of moral high
ground with me, Dorrek—for if your heart was truly
Klingon, you would obey the order I am about to give."

"You order me?" Dorrek laughed at that, a bitter,
angry sound. *"By what right?"*

"As your older brother. Whether you like it or
not, I am head of our House, and that gives me *every*
right to instruct you. Now, in the name of the House
of M'Raq, I order you to join us. Face the general
down. Remember that a Klingon's word is his bond,
and without it, we are *nothing*."

*"My duty, brother, is to obey the orders of my superi-
ors. That is something you will never be."* Dorrek shook
his head, and seemed to look away. *"I had hoped to
end this without having to kill my own brother, but you
will not spare our House even this indignity. You will not
deviate from this path of dishonor that will lead us both to
the Barge of the Dead for eternity."* He looked back at
Klag. *"I will see you in Gre'thor, Klag."*

He cut the transmission off.

Klag sat and stared at the bulkheads—for how
long, he knew not.

"Bridge to Klag."

Several seconds passed before Klag finally acknowledged Kornan's voice.

"The fleet will be in firing range in three minutes."

Realizing he'd been staring at the bulkheads for entirely too long, he said, "I will be on the bridge shortly."

Klag got up. He stumbled to the right as he did so, and then slammed his fist into his desk.

"I would speak with you."

Kurak turned to see Lokor standing in the entryway to the engineering section, his arms folded across his broad chest. The chief engineer knew the head of security by reputation, though she had never met him until today. She had seen him, of course—with his lengthy, intricately braided hair, he was impossible to miss—but his presence had never been required in her area of responsibility, and she hardly went out of her way to socialize.

"Lieutenant, we are about to go into battle," Kurak said impatiently. "Can't this wait?"

"It is precisely because we are about to go into battle that we must have this conversation now."

Letting out a long breath between her teeth, Kurak walked over to him, gripping her right wrist with her left hand. "Speak then, but do it quickly. I have little patience."

"Which is part of the problem." He swept one massive arm—uncovered, as Lokor was wearing a sleeveless tunic—toward the engineers scattering about their posts. "All the warriors on this ship are behind the captain. They know that his cause is just and honorable. Even those who do not agree with him follow him because it is their duty, even though it may mean death for us all.

"In fact, they are convinced that they *will* die because they know how hopeless our cause is. We are outnumbered, and Talak can call upon the resources of the entire fleet. The captain, at best, can depend upon what few members of the Order of the *Bat'leth* truly feel the siren call of honor in their blood." Lokor smiled, a most unpleasant expression. "I have observed you to be a realist, Commander, so I think you would agree with me that truly honorable warriors in the Empire are few and far between."

If I gave it any consideration whatsoever, I would, Kurak thought, but did not say so aloud. Interrupting Lokor would only make him take that much longer to finish what he was saying and go away.

"What is required in this engagement is innovation. The subspace eddies have required us to glean new ways of—"

Now Kurak did interrupt because she knew what Lokor would say. "I have already had this conversation with Klag, with Kornan, with Toq, and with the imbeciles under my command, Lieutenant. I will not tolerate it from you as well."

The smile fell. "I will be the judge of what will be tolerated on this ship when it comes to the welfare of the troops. Right now, Commander, you are a liability because you refuse to do everything necessary to achieve victory. If we are to win this day, we must find a way for *all* our weapons to function in this mad space. Not only will it give us a tactical advantage, but it will say to the troops—who have beamed down to San-Tarah fully expecting to die in a futile gesture of honor—that we are doing all we can to win. Without that, the soldiers will simply go through the motions. But a warrior inspired to fight is a great thing indeed, and I believe that the warriors of this ship will shine given the chance. As the officers go, so go the troops. If they see you attempting to better our position, they will do the same." Lokor walked forward, and loomed over Kurak. He stood a full head and a half taller than her, and his long braids fell menacingly down over his shoulders, like *wam* serpents preparing to strike. "If, on the other hand, you continue with the same disregard for your duties that you have displayed since we left the shipping yards, then we *will* lose this battle. I find this unacceptable. Therefore, you will do everything you can to achieve this goal, Commander."

"Or what?" Kurak spoke dismissively. "You are beneath both my notice and my contempt, *Lieutenant*, and you have no authority over me. Now if you're quite finished, I—"

"Authority is nothing without power and resources, *Commander*," Lokor said, not sounding at all dismissed. "After all, Captain Klag has no authority over General Talak, yet he uses the power of his convictions and the resources of the Order of the *Bat'leth* to do what is right." Then the smile came back. "If you imagine that, as security chief of this ship, I am without either of those things, you are very much mistaken."

"Killing me will not accomplish your goal, Lieutenant."

"Nothing was said about killing, Commander," Lokor said in a gentle tone that concerned Kurak more than a belligerent tone would have. "And with reason. As you rightly point out, killing you will not accomplish my goal." He stood upright. "You will not be with us much longer, will you? Once your nephew enters his officer training, you will resign."

Lokor's knowledge of this did not surprise Kurak. Though she had not advertised the fact, she did not make a secret of it, either. "Yes."

"The House of Palkar must always serve the Empire." Lokor's knowledge of her family's pet phrase *did* surprise Kurak, but she said nothing as he continued. "Which means his entry into the Defense Force will free you to resign your commission and return to whatever civilian pursuits you occupied yourself with before others of your House were so inconsiderate as to die." Lokor fixed his pitiless brown eyes on Kurak. "But what, I wonder, would you do if something happened to prevent your nephew from completing his training—or not even starting it?"

A cold sensation started in Kurak's heart and spread to her entire chest. She found she could not feel her feet.

Lokor went on. "That would necessitate your remaining in the Defense Force for, what—three more years, at least?"

Kurak said nothing. She did not dare.

Baring his teeth in a manner similar to that of a *tri-*

gak about to pounce, Lokor said, "We will not speak of this again, Commander. Because we will not have to."

With that, he turned and left engineering.

Kurak stared after him.

But she did not see Lokor's retreating form. She saw the long face of Moloj, the *gIntaq* for the House of Palkar, on the viewscreen of her office at the Science Institute on Mempa V.

She had been in the midst of a delicate experiment, as she and her team were very close to figuring out a way to increase the efficiency of the antimatter injectors in the smaller warp drives that shuttles and other low-personnel vehicles used. She hadn't wanted to take the communication—when they were done, she was scheduled to go sailing on the lake outside the institute, something she had been promising herself for months and had finally secured the leave time to indulge in—but she knew better than to refuse Moloj. If it was something she could ignore, Moloj would have had one of his servants take care of the call; Moloj himself meant important family business.

"What do you want?" she had asked him then.

"Your father has requested that you return to the Homeworld immediately."

That took Kurak aback. "For what reason?"

"Does it matter?" Moloj's disdain came through the viewer quite clearly. He had never approved of Kurak's choice to become a scientist and researcher. The House of Palkar was, after all, laden with heroes of the Defense Force, and Moloj could not under-

stand why she would desire anything other than to follow in their footsteps.

"Yes, it does. I'm in the midst of delicate—"

"*I'm sure that whatever vile experiments you are performing may seem vital, but—*"

Kurak snarled. "My experiments are designed to increase the performance of the engines that your *precious* warriors use in battle! Even a fool with as limited vision as you have, old man, should be able to see *that*."

Moloj had a small white beard that mostly served to hide the fact that he had no discernible chin. What little chin he had, however, twisted as Moloj obviously struggled to control his reaction. When she was a girl, Kurak used to enjoy teasing the usually unflappable *gIntaq*, to try to get some kind of reaction. As an adult, she had nothing but contempt for him, and tried to get a similar reaction mainly because she simply didn't care.

She did not succeed, however. Instead, he looked away briefly, looked back at the viewer, and said, "*Your father has requested that you return to the Homeworld immediately. The House transport will be arriving at Mempa V within the day. You will leave with it.*"

Realizing there was nothing to gain by arguing, except for the perverse satisfaction of angering Moloj—which was not worth the effort—Kurak agreed. With irritation and regret, she cancelled her sailing jaunt, and then spent the rest of the day putting her affairs in order. The latter primarily consisted of explaining the situation to Makros. Luckily, her supervisor understood the dilemma. The House of Palkar was powerful, and one did not refuse the summons of so influential a House Head as Kurak's father.

When she arrived at the Palkar estates on Qo'noS, Moloj greeted her at the door. "The captain is in his office."

"The captain," Kurak thought. *Very subtle, Moloj.*

Father kept his black hair relatively short. He had small, slanted eyes that were almost hidden under his elaborate crest. He sat at a massive wooden desk that was covered with padds and a workstation. The desk had been carved from a tree that had been at the center of the site on which the estate now sat.

After Moloj let her into the office, Kurak stood before her father. He didn't even look up at her arrival, but continued working on one padd in particular. Then he put it down, picked up another, read it briefly, set it down, then, finally, looked up at his eldest daughter.

"I am reporting to Ty'Gokor tomorrow to take command of my fleet." Father spoke in as straightforward a tone as Moloj had the previous day. "You will join me and enlist in the Defense Force. I assume that you would be of use as some kind of engineer."

Kurak blinked. "Father, I—"

"The House of Palkar must—"

" '—always serve the Empire,' yes, I *know,* Father!" She could not believe this—and yet she had no trouble believing it. Moloj, after all, wasn't the only one who looked upon her chosen profession with disdain. "You might recall that I designed Gowron's flagship. If that does not constitute serving the Empire, then—"

"We leave at first sun. That is all."

Then he picked up another padd and activated its display.

"Father, there is no need for this. My brothers, you, Mother, Grandmother—what more needs to be proven? I am a valued member of Makros's staff, and I have—"

Looking back up, Father said, "It is not a question of what needs to be 'proven.' Since the days of Emperor Sompek, our House has served the Empire. You have been permitted your dalliance with the sciences because our House is well represented in the Defense Force, but things have changed. We are now at war with the Dominion, and we *all* must do *everything* we can. That is why you will accompany me to Ty'Gokor tomorrow." He looked back down at his padd. "That is all."

Through clenched teeth, Kurak said, "I *do* serve, Father, don't you understand that—"

Now Father didn't even bother to look up. "That is all, daughter. You will leave me now. If you do not accompany me tomorrow, you will be discommendated from this House."

Her jaw fell open in stupefaction. Discommendation from House Palkar would completely cut her off from any further job opportunities at her current level. Makros would not be able to have her on staff in any serious capacity, and she would not be permitted to take any kind of position of responsibility in her field.

"This is how you maintain the honor of our House, then, is it, Father? Through threats and extortion?"

He still did not look up. "You have given me no choice. Moloj will take care of your needs until morning."

Kurak stared at the top of her father's head for several seconds before finally turning and departing his office.

As expected, Moloj waited outside the door and led her to her rooms. They hadn't changed in the ten years since she'd last set foot in them. Indeed, Moloj's staff had maintained them perfectly. She resisted a very strong urge to set fire to the place.

The next day she and Father flew in silence to Ty'Gokor. Makros's influence was enough to convince the higher-ups in the Defense Force to grant her the field rank of commander and place her on the *Lallek* as chief engineer.

She'd never been more miserable in her life. The mistake she made was in thinking that this was as bad as it could get.

Two years later, the *Lallek* was part of the task force that took Cardassia Prime. Kurak had eschewed the honor of joining Chancellor Martok and the Starfleet and Romulan officers who toured the charred remains of the planet. Instead, she had gone to her quarters to pack. The war was now over. The death toll had been tremendous: Makros died in a Breen attack on a shipyard, and Father's fleet was destroyed at Avinall VII. Her brothers and grandparents were also killed in battle, and were probably now all serving on the same ship in *Sto-Vo-Kor* that the others of their House served on, gloating about how well they had served the Empire over the centuries. Kurak's mother, Haleka, still served as a *QaS DevwI'* on the *Kri'stak*, and could damn well carry on the family tradition without her. She hated the way the Defense Force operated, the way she was ordered like some kind of servant, the way she was expected to perform tasks without any proper tests or decent laboratory conditions. It was appalling, and it made her wonder how the Empire ever managed to win any victories.

Her packing was interrupted by a communication from Moloj. She no more wanted to take it now than she had two years earlier, but she also knew it would be futile not to.

Moloj's hair had grown whiter in so short a time, but he otherwise had the same dull, long face. "*Your mother is dead.*"

Almost by habit, Kurak said, "I'm sure she died with honor."

Then the realization hit her with the force of a quantum torpedo.

They're all dead.

"*Young Gevnar has not come of age yet. He will not be able to begin his officer training for another two years.*"

Kurak said nothing. She gripped her right wrist so hard she thought all blood would cease flowing in her right arm, but she said nothing.

"Of course, you could petition the High Council for special dispensation to be made House Head. Then you would not be forced to remain in the Defense Force." Moloj actually smiled when he said that. Kurak had never seen Moloj smile, and decided she didn't like it much.

"I'm sure," she said through gritted teeth, "that you know damn well that I would sooner dive naked into a vat of hungry *taknar* than be forced to become administrator of our House. You are welcome to perform that task until Gevnar's Age of Ascension, Moloj, believe me."

"Just so. Which means you must remain in the Defense Force. Your father made that quite clear before he went on to Sto-Vo-Kor. You will serve, or you will be discommendated."

The next week, she was transferred to the *Gorkon*.

"Commander?"

Shaking her head, Kurak came back to the present. Lokor had long since left the engine room. She turned to see one of the idiots under her command trying to get her attention. "What?"

"The intermix chamber is fluctuating again."

"Then *fix* it!" Kurak snapped. "I have work to do." The engineer scampered off.

Kurak then went to one of the weapons consoles. She needed to find a way to get the disruptors to fire amid the subspace eddies.

She had already lost the one thing she enjoyed besides her work on this mission when Kornan and the rest of the *petaQ* on this mad vessel ruined her love of sailing. Now this.

Perhaps Lokor was bluffing; he was, after all, just a Defense Force lieutenant from a minor House. What could he possibly do to Gevnar, the eldest son of as strong a House as Palkar?

No, that one is not the kind who bluffs. The Defense Force may be littered with fools and imbeciles, but not liars and deceivers. Lokor would not make the threat if he did not intend to follow through on it, any more than Father would have hesitated to cast me out.

So she went to work on the disruptors.

On board the bridge of the *Akua*, General Talak sat at the edge of his command chair. "Scan the subspace eddies—find the other ships. We'll pick away Klag's support first, then take on his ship."

"Aye, sir," the operations officer said.

Talak looked at his status board. He could feel the roar of blood in his veins. Even though it was fellow Klingons he was taking on, it was still battle. *This is what we were born for.*

"We've detected the *Slivin* and the *Vidd*."

Talak grinned. "Excellent!" He examined the status board, saw that two of the *Karas*-class ships were in position to attack those ships. "Send in the *Vornar* and the *Kalpak*."

"The *Gorkon* is taking up a defensive posture within the eddies, sir."

"Send Captain Huss after him. Have the *K'mpec* plot an orbital course and prepare to send down troops to secure the planet." *I won't force a warrior to fire on his own brother unless I have to.* "Are photon torpedoes still online?"

"Yes, sir." The operations officer grinned. "The technique we obtained was quite successful."

"Good. We have neutralized every advantage Klag *thinks* he has." Klag was a fool to believe that every member of the Order would follow his lead. Martok's pretty speeches notwithstanding, the Order was an all-night party and a medallion and not much else. Worse, the captain had been stupid enough to trust *all* those who answered his call, unable to even conceive of treachery, so blinded was he by his imagined honor.

The general stared at the viewscreen, which showed the two *Karas*-class ships heading toward the eddies. The disruptions in subspace were not visible to the naked eye as such—only their effect was. Talak could not see the planet that he knew was only a few thousand *qell'qams* away. The viewscreen's image translator defaulted to the visible spectrum. "Overlay the subspace eddies on the screen," Talak said. "I want—"

Before he could specify what he wanted, he saw an explosion only a few *qell'qams* off the bows of the two ships. Fire plumed outward in all directions, consuming most of the *Vornar* and a good portion of the *Kalpak*.

Talak was on his feet like a shot. "Report!"

The operations officer was scanning her console, trying to do that very thing. "Some kind of explosive device," she said redundantly. "It must have been hidden in the eddies."

"Why were we not warned of this?" Talak asked, knowing that there was no answer. *Obviously Klag did not share all his intelligence with his fleet. It would seem I did not give him enough credit.*

I will not make that mistake again.

"Sir, the *Jor* and the *Nukmay* are showing damage—they must have struck one of the eddies. The *Gorkon* is taking an evasive course." The officer looked up and smiled. "Sir, it is taking them directly on course for the *Gro'kan!*"

That was one of the *K'Vort*-class ships, the other being the *Tagak*. "Good. Have the *Tagak* come about and hem them in. Have Huss regroup and seek out the other ships."

"*K'mpec* reports ground troops beamed down successfully."

Talak smiled. The Chancellor-class ships had fifteen hundred ground troops assigned, and the general had thousands more troops in reserve on the *Akua* if they could not hold it. *Now Dorrek can show his brother how to truly conquer a world.*

Another explosion caught his attention, this one damaging both the *Tagak* and the *Gro'kan*. "Another mine, sir. The *Gorkon* took damage as well, but the other ships' shields are tattered."

Enough of this. Talak sat back down in his chair. "Attack posture—we will destroy the *Gorkon* ourselves! Full impulse!"

The operations officer leaned forward. "Sir, we still do not know how many of these explosives there are—or where they are located, or how much damage they can—"

Before she could finish that thought, another explosion lit up the status board. "On screen!" Talak bellowed.

This time it wasn't a mine—it was the *Vornar* exploding, taking the hulk of the *Kalpak* with it. *Whatever that mine was, it was enough to cause the* Vornar's *warp core to breach.*

"Reverse course!"

That surprised the pilot. "Sir?"

Talak turned to the operations officer. "We will hold back for the time being. I want every resource on this ship geared toward finding those mines and neutralizing them." Talak had not expected to lose two ships so quickly—in fact, given the numerical advantage, he had not expected to lose any ships at all. Aside from the *Taj* and the two Chancellor-class ships, and Talak's own ship, of course, the *Karas*-class vessels were the most heavily armed in this engagement—they had a torpedo complement far in excess of the other like-sized ships—and they were also smaller and more maneuverable than the others. Losing two-thirds of them...

"Yes, sir," the operations officer said, and started madly working her console.

Angrily, Talak watched as the *Gorkon*'s photon torpedoes started plowing through the hulls of both the *Gro'kan* and the *Tagak*. The latter two ships' torpedo cannons had been damaged, leaving them vulnerable. *That's two more.*

"The *Slivin* has engaged the *K'mpec* in orbit," came a report from the pilot. The officer then laughed. "It is a good day for them to die, sir—the *Slivin* has been destroyed."

Finally. "They will not be the last to fall. That, I swear."

CHAPTER SIX

Blood spurted in all directions as Ga-Tror sliced the head off the Klingon. Then he turned to face another. Ga-Tror's fur was matted with the blood of his enemies; his tongue was hanging out the side of his mouth with the exertions of battle.

He thought this would be more fun.

Not that the joys of fighting more Klingons didn't fill him with glee. Today's fight made the Great Hunt seem like a chasing off of a minor predator from one's hut. But the words of Leader Wol and *QaS DevwI'* Vok from days earlier—which, in turn, mirrored words spoken by Te-Run on the eve of Me-Larr's final fight in the circle against Captain Klag—still preyed on his mind. When Te-Run had warned them of the dangers of aliens like the Klingons coming to San-Tarah in the future, the Fight Leader had dismissed her words as the ramblings of an old woman.

But Leader Wol and *QaS DevwI'* Vok's attempts to explain the universe outside their world did what Te-Run could not—show Ga-Tror how limited his perspective truly was.

Two of the enemy Klingons sliced at Ga-Tror with their small knives; he believed they were called *daktags*. Ga-Tror almost laughed instead of defending the attack. However, it was the work of only a few moments to disarm both of them with his two-bladed sword. Then, with one downward slice, he was able to cut through one Klingon's neck while kicking at the other. His toe claws were unable to penetrate the Klingon's armor, but the blow staggered his foe long enough for Ga-Tror to remove his sword from one neck and impale the other's chest with it.

He looked around. Ga-Tror was part of the group that defended the Prime Village against the two hundred troops the enemy Klingons had sent to take it. Captain Klag had sent only one hundred of his own troops for the main part of the village, but supplemented them with thirty Children of San-Tarah, led by Ga-Tror.

The *Gorkon* troops were holding their own, as were the Children of San-Tarah. At least, that was how it appeared. In all honesty, Ga-Tror had difficulty telling the different Klingons apart. They all wore the same uniforms, and—especially in the midst of a fight—they seemed a blend of undistinguished flat-faced, furless bipeds.

Ga-Tror stood right now in front of one of the residential huts; he wasn't sure whose, and it didn't matter. Le-Rak and Leader Wol were fighting off three other Klingons in front of the hut next to that. Ga-Tror ran to give aid. Just as a Klingon sword cut through Le-Rak's right arm, Ga-Tror leapt and kicked another Klingon to the ground. Before the enemy could recover, Ga-Tror slammed his sword into the Klingon's chest.

Sharp pain sliced into his side, and Ga-Tror whirled around, slashing with his claws. They struck the face of another Klingon, who had shoved his knife into Ga-Tror. The Klingon staggered backward, losing his grip on the knife. Ga-Tror ripped the knife from his side and threw it unerringly at the stumbling Klingon's ridged forehead.

Without waiting to see if his foe fell, he turned back and removed his sword from the first, just as Leader Wol cut through the arm of one of her enemies. That arm held a weapon, and Ga-Tror came to Leader Wol's aid by slicing off the head of the stunned Klingon.

Leader Wol nodded her head. Ga-Tror knew that this was an acknowledgment of some sort to the Klingons.

Le-Rak said, "We are winning the fight."

Ga-Tror looked around. The corpses of many Klingons—and many Children of San-Tarah—lined the ground. He saw groups of as many as two or three combined *Gorkon* Klingons and Children of San-Tarah fighting single Klingons. Blood stained the dirt and grass. Many fine fighters ran with the dead now.

The Fight Leader ran toward the center of the Prime Village. Two members of the Ruling Pack, Ya-Mar and Tre-Sor, as well as Leader Avok of the *Gorkon*, were battling seven Klingons. Ya-Mar bled profusely from several wounds, but she continued to fight. Her sword sliced through the belly of one Klingon even as she fell forward. Tre-Sor defended against two of the Klingon curved weapons—*bat-letts*, they were called, or something like that—while Leader Avok was being overwhelmed by the other four.

Ga-Tror and Le-Rak attacked the ones harassing Leader Avok, making short work of them. Leader Avok himself impaled one Klingon even as the other sliced open his throat with a larger knife. Ga-Tror grabbed the latter by the hair, yanked her downward, and ripped out her throat with his claws.

They had been fighting for most of the day. Ga-Tror's initial assessment of the Klingons was that they were dilettantes. They claimed to be "warriors," but had only limited combat skills. Some were better than others, of course, but they were, overall, lacking.

Now he realized that he had misjudged them. The reason the initial attack from the *Gorkon* had failed was not because they were poor fighters, but because the Children of San-Tarah were better than expected. Had Captain Klag not agreed to the contests, he would have sent down more fighters.

The result would be the carnage they had now. Worse, really, for they would not have the aid they were receiving from Captain Klag's troops.

He looked at Le-Rak. "Where is Leader Wol?"

"She rejoined her squadron." He looked around. "I think we've won."

"We've won nothing," Ga-Tror said. "We have defended the Prime Village, but this day's fight will not be over for some time."

Te-Run ran up to where they stood. To Ga-Tror's glee, she was as covered in Klingon gore as the rest of them. *She may be old, but she still has plenty of fight in her.*

"Bring those that are wounded to the Meeting Hut. Dr. B'Oraq has set up a healing center there."

"A what?"

"She calls it a *hospa-tal,* whatever that means. There, she will be able to heal those that are wounded."

Le-Rak's mouth fell open. "She can make my arm whole?"

"Possibly."

Ga-Tror had heard that the Klingons had great healing arts. He had even seen evidence of it in Lieutenant Toq, who had received wounds gained when hunting the *san-chera* that should have taken most of a season to recover from.

"You were right," Ga-Tror said to Te-Run even as Le-Rak limped to the Meeting Hut.

"I am often right," Te-Run said archly. "The fact that you do not acknowledge this is the main thing that holds you back, Ga-Tror."

At that, Ga-Tror laughed. "Perhaps. But I refer specifically to your words to the Ruling Pack about the future of our people. Casting out the Klingons may doom us."

"I wouldn't worry," Te-Run said. "Casting them out doesn't seem to have worked very well. And we all may run with the dead before this is all over."

Looking out at the number who already did so, Ga-Tror said grimly, "You may be right. Never have so many died in one fight before."

"And the fight has only begun. But we fight for our world. If we all must die, then we will die. There are no alternatives."

Ga-Tror looked down. "*QaS DevwI'* Vok told me of a concept that I did not understand: *surrender*. There are those in the universe that will give up— that will concede without even giving a proper fight. I cannot imagine anything more disgusting."

Te-Run laughed. "I, too, was introduced to this by Captain Klag. It is an option that only presents itself to those who are faced with a superior foe. Until the Klingons came, we never faced a superior foe. But it is still not an option. This is our world. It was chosen for us and we for it. They cannot take it from us, and they will not."

The air then spoke. "*Vok to Ga-Tror.*"

Startled, Ga-Tror took a moment to recall that *QaS DevwI'* Vok had given the Fight Leader one of their communications tools. "Yes?"

"*The main road is secure.*"

"As is the Prime Village. So far, we are victorious."

"*It won't last. And several other villages have fallen or*

*are falling. We may need to redistribute our own troops
to try to take the villages back or better defend them."*

Ga-Tror's vision swam. He remembered the
wound in his side. "We will gather at the Meeting
Hut and determine how this will be done."

"Agreed. I'll meet you there shortly."

Though there was always fighting, this was the
first war in Ga-Tror's lifetime—and the first pro-
longed war in the history of the Children of San-
Tarah, for their previous skirmishes all were short.
The victories had always been decisive. He doubted
that would be the case this time.

"Come," he said to Te-Run, "let us see if Dr. B'Oraq
can wield her Klingon magic on my wounds."

Leaving Le-Rak and Ga-Tror to aid Avok and the
two members of the Ruling Pack, Leader Wol ran off
in search of the rest of the fifteenth. The search
didn't take long: all she had to do was seek out
Goran's immense form. Sure enough, the massive
bekk was taking on several of the *K'mpec*'s ground
troops at once, and not even getting scratched. He
was also grinning so widely, Wol thought his face
would crack open. Wol was grateful, as Goran's loss
of the strength contest had driven the soldier to a literally suicidal depression. G'joth and Wol had refused to perform the *Mauk-to'Vor* ritual on him, and
had talked him out of finding another to kill him
with honor. As she had hoped, a good dose of carnage cheered Goran right up.

Maris and Trant were being harried by four troops. Wol ran toward them, only to have the two facing Maris run off.

Wol looked around to see that a general retreat appeared to have been called—not surprising, as the *K'mpec*'s troops never had a serious chance in the Prime Village. The two fighting Trant, however, had apparently not gotten the call, or felt that killing Trant was more important. Wol had spent enough time with Trant to believe the latter quite likely.

One of Trant's foes fell rather suddenly, and Trant stabbed the other in the neck just as Wol arrived. The first Klingon fell forward, a familiar-looking *qut-luch* in his back.

G'joth approached. Wol smiled. "I was wondering what happened to Davok's prized knife."

"Well," G'joth said with a grin as he yanked the assassin's weapon out of the back of Trant's enemy, "I could hardly let it go to waste."

Trant shook his head. "This is wrong."

"What is?" Wol asked.

Gesturing to the entire Prime Village. "All of this. Klingons should not be fighting Klingons." Sweeping his gesture down to the two Children of San-Tarah who lay dead at his feet with *d'k tahg*s impaling their persons, Trant added, "Certainly not alongside outsiders. We should be united against our enemies, not squabbling with each other like brawlers in a tavern. We are above such things."

"I don't know what makes me more ill, Trant,

your self-righteous posturing, or your stupidity." G'joth's voice was dripping with a contempt that the old *toDSaH* usually reserved for the late Davok. "Klingons *always* fight Klingons. Klingons have always *fought* Klingons. And Klingons always *will* fight Klingons. Sometimes it's noble Houses in conflict or civil war. It was only a few months ago that Klingon fought Klingon during the coup attempt on Martok after the war. Before that, there was House Duras's attempt to depose Gowron before he could ascend to the chancellorship." G'joth laughed. "It's what we do best."

Trant growled, and his hand went to his *d'k tahg*.

"Are you going to challenge me, Trant?" G'joth asked. "Wouldn't that require that you fight a fellow Klingon?"

The growl mutated into a huff, and Trant then turned and hobbled off. Only then did Wol realize that his leg was injured. She debated telling him to report to the *HoSpI'tal* that B'Oraq had set up, then decided that it wasn't worth it. *If he wants to heal himself, he knows where to go. If he does not, then he will die and be out of my squadron.*

Maris simply stood there. Wol looked at him. "I notice you've been very quiet, Maris."

Smiling, Maris said, "The last time I spoke in response to something Trant said, it set a chain of events in motion that led to my being demoted. I'd prefer to avoid anything worse happening in the future."

"Very wise," Wol said.

"*Vok to Wol.*"

Pressing the communicator on her wrist, the Leader replied, "Wol."

"*We have secured the Prime Village and the road. However, two other villages will need additional troops. The village of Val-Goral has fallen to the enemy—and they have set up transporter blockers, so we cannot beam in.*"

Wol started. "They have managed to make transporter blockers work?" The first thing the *Gorkon* crew had attempted days ago was to get transporter blockers to function, but they wouldn't work any better than hand scanners or disruptors.

"*Yes—I want Fifteenth through Twentieth Squads to go to Val-Goral and take it back. The squads there are still fighting, but they're contained. We need a fresh attack from the outside.*"

"Who will lead the battle, you or *QaS DevwI'* Klaris?" The assigned squads were from both troop commanders' ranks.

"*Neither. Klaris will be leading Twenty-first through Thirtieth Squads to supplement our forces at Val-Terin. We are losing ground there, and we need to begin our marine attack.*"

Wol remembered that Val-Terin was the site of the largest dock along the Great Sea. Me-Larr had proposed using wind boats as a supplemental attack force from that village, armed with *tal-lyns* and some other upgrades from *Gorkon* engineers. But, perhaps recognizing this, Klag's brother had sent more troops there than even to the Prime Village, and so the *Gorkon* troops and the Children of San-Tarah were having trouble holding the village.

"So who will lead us?"

"You, Leader Wol."

Imagining Vok's cheerful grin as he spoke, Wol found her own jaw falling open. "Me?"

"You lead the first among the assigned squads. To whom else would I give the honor?"

Wol resisted the urge to say, "Almost anyone else."

"Assemble the troops and leave immediately, Leader. Your main objective is to capture those transporter blockers."

Many thoughts ran through Wol's head, most of them wondering whether or not Vok had suffered some kind of cranial trauma to put her in charge. But all she said was "Understood, *QaS DevwI'*."

Then she sent Maris after Trant. They had work to do.

"Incoming transmission from the *Vidd* on the coded frequency," Toq said from behind Klag.

The captain smiled. He'd been expecting this. "On screen. Grint, another spread on the *Tagak*."

Klag had been careful: the *Gorkon* had left Ty'Gokor with a full complement of one hundred and two photon torpedoes, and had used none of them prior to today's battle, but they still needed to ration them, as they were the only available weapons. To his irritation—but not his surprise, given Dorrek's prior knowledge of Klag's fleet of Order ships—his enemy also had use of photons.

The image on the viewscreen changed from six torpedoes making short work of the *Tagak*'s secondary hull to that of K'Vada. "*I was wondering, Captain, when you were planning to inform the rest of us of those mines.*"

"You were informed when the first one exploded. The courses I gave you to follow were very specific, and avoided encountering any of them."

"*I swore fealty to you, Captain. I don't appreciate being lied to.*"

"You weren't. I never said there weren't any mines."

"*Such semantic trickery—you sound like a human.*"

Letting the insult pass, Klag leaned forward. "Captain, you may have observed that our foes are firing torpedoes even with the subspace interference. That means that we have a traitor in our midst, and it behooves me to be parsimonious with intelligence. That is my right as leader of this battle. If you wish to challenge that—"

"*Of course not,*" K'Vada said quickly. "*I just hope your other surprises continue to benefit us and not the general. Out.*"

As K'Vada's face faded from the viewer, Klag ordered a tactical overlay.

The *Tagak* was dead in space, and the *Gro'tak* had been destroyed. That left six ships in the general's fleet—and only two of them, the *K'mpec* and the *Gogam*, were actually engaged in battle. Captain Huss's three birds-of-prey were going through the subspace eddies, apparently trying to ferret out the mines, and General Talak was hanging back in reserve.

But Klag had lost the *Slivin*, and the *Ch'marq* and the *Qovin* were badly damaged. The *Taj* was engaged with the *Gogam*—the last of the *Karas*-class strike ships—but neither ship was making much headway, trying as they were to conserve torpedoes and avoid the damaging subspace eddies. The *K'mpec* was making short work of the *Ch'marq* and *Qovin*.

With his own foes down, that left Klag to either come to the aid of the *Qovin* and the *Ch'marq* against Dorrek, help the *Taj* against the *Gogam*, or take the *Akua*.

While he contemplated, Kornan said, "Grint, fire one torpedo on the *Tagak*."

Klag nodded his approval. It wouldn't do to waste more than one torpedo, and in the state the *Tagak* was in, that would be sufficient to destroy it. They could not risk keeping the enemy alive so they could effect repairs and rejoin the battle. Better to send them to *Sto-Vo-Kor* as quickly and efficiently as possible.

The *Qovin* and the *Ch'marq* needed his help the most. *Especially*, Klag thought, *since Daqset never swore fealty to me. He may well be the traitor.*

No, he finally decided, *I will not fire on my brother*. And Captain B'Edra, he knew, could take care of herself. That left the third option.

To Kornan, he said, "It is time the general joined the battle that he has begun. We will lure him into the eddies."

"Yes, sir." Kornan rose and looked at Grint. "Fire two torpedoes on the *Akua*."

Klag turned to the pilot's position. "Leskit, plot the most direct course to San-Tarah."

Leskit whirled around. "That would involve the most maneuvering."

"Yes, and you've had five days to perfect the art of such maneuvers. I doubt that the general's pilot will be so proficient."

Laughing, Leskit said, "I should hope not. Setting course."

"Minimal damage to the *Akua*," Grint reported.

Toq added, "They are changing course to intercept and have locked their own torpedoes."

"Execute course," Kornan said, "half impulse."

Klag gave his first officer an approving nod. He would have been content with quarter impulse—in that labyrinth out there, it would be enough of a challenge—but he preferred the more aggressive posture.

The captain clenched his father's former fist in appreciation. *The battle goes better than expected.* Rodek's mines had done their work well, taking out two of the enemy before the battle even started. The numbers were closer to even, and Klag had important advantages: superior knowledge of the territory, for one thing, and the cause of honor. *It may be a good day to die, but it is a better day to win.*

"*Akua* is pursuing on an intercept course with us," Toq said. "They're firing."

The torpedoes collided with the *Gorkon*'s shields even as both ships continued wending their way toward the planet. "Shields down to seventy-five percent," Grint said. "They're firing again."

"Aft torpedoes, lock on and return fire," Kornan said.

Klag's eyes remained fixed on the viewscreen, which showed the *Akua* moving closer. "Speed of the *Akua*?"

"Full impulse," Toq said.

Throwing his head back, Klag laughed. "The general is a bigger fool than I thought. He risks—"

The *Akua*'s course changed suddenly. A piece of their left wing exploded, though the debris was not visible.

"Report!" Kornan barked. Klag, however, suspected the answer.

Toq said, "The *Akua*'s port wing has crossed into one of the subspace eddies. Their shields are down!"

"Fire torpedoes!" Klag and Kornan both barked.

Just as Grint did so, a collision alarm went off.

"I've lost helm control!" Leskit said.

"We've also hit an eddy, sir," Toq said. "Damage to aft hull. Shields and cloak are offline. Structural-integrity field is failing!"

"I've regained helm control," Leskit said with remarkable calm. "Resuming course."

Several consoles in the aft section exploded. "Torpedo impact with the neck!" Grint cried over the alarms.

"Structural-integrity field down to fourteen percent!"

"Sir," Kornan said, looking down at his own console, "the *Taj!*"

Klag whirled on his first officer. "What about it?"

"It *and* the *Gogam* are changing course!"

"On screen!"

Looking to the viewer, Klag saw both ships—in formation—heading into orbit of San-Tarah.

Toq said, "They are on an intercept course for the *K'mpec's* position, sir."

A moment later, they had achieved orbit—and *both* ships fired in tandem on both the *Qovin* and the *Ch'marq.* The bird-of-prey exploded in a fiery conflagration, and the *Ch'marq's* running lights dimmed to almost nothing, its hull pocked with breaches.

Ten weeks ago, B'Edra had praised Klag's prowess at Narendra III and toasted B'Oraq's medical accomplishments. Klag had classified her as the one among his allies to be the most trustworthy.

And she has betrayed me.

Kornan looked up. "Sir, the *Taj* is beaming ground troops to the surface of San-Tarah."

"Structural-integrity field down to ten percent," Toq added.

Now Klag pounded the arm of his chair with his right fist. *The battle is no longer going better than expected. . . .*

CHAPTER SEVEN

G'joth lay on his belly and began to understand why taking Val-Goral was going to be a challenge.

The village was located in a valley that was accessible only by sea (north and west) or via a steep incline with no cover (east and south). Along with the other members of the fifteenth, G'joth was positioned at the top of one of the southern inclines, looking down on Val-Goral. He could see several Klingons setting up a command post, the bodies of many Klingons and Children of San-Tarah lining the ground, and isolated pockets of fighting.

G'joth suspected that Me-Larr had assured the *QaS DevwI'* that they would have little trouble defending this place, and so did not send sufficient troops to defend it. Or, rather, the number of troops would have been sufficient if not for transporter technology. While a direct assault would be anticipated by virtue of the steep approach, the troops that arrived from the *K'mpec* could just beam into the village.

The transporter blockers meant that the *Gorkon* troops could not use the same tactics. *Luckily, we don't have to.*

Next to him, Leader Wol activated her communicator, which was on a coded frequency that Lieutenant Toq had developed for use among those fighting on the side of the Order of the *Bat'leth.* "Eighteenth, Nineteenth, and Twentieth Squads, prepare for frontal assault." Those three squads were positioned at the easternmost part of the incline. "The rest, prepare grenades."

G'joth grinned. His idea to make grenades had worked out spectacularly. They required only material found on San-Tarah or on the *Gorkon,* and were chemical in nature, and therefore not susceptible to the vicissitudes of the subspace eddies.

Each grenade was a hollow metal oval, into which they had placed the sand from the shores of the Prime Village and a small glass bottle containing *ngIS*—a lubricant used on the disruptor cannons, and which the *Gorkon* had in plentiful supply. Throwing the grenade with sufficient force would break the bottle upon impact with a solid surface— they had been using B'Oraq's specimen bottles, which were fairly fragile—causing an explosive chemical reaction with one of the minerals in the sand.

Wol continued. "Focus grenade barrage on the command center."

"Leader," Trant said, "I noticed something."

"You're an idiot?" G'joth muttered.

"I'm sure the *bekk*'s observation is less blindingly obvious," Wol said dryly. "What is it, Trant?"

Baring his teeth in a snarl at G'joth, Trant then turned back to the Leader. "Several of the warriors below are armed with some kind of old-fashioned projectile weapon."

Wol nodded. "Yes, I saw that. They look like a human device called a *QoSbow*." She laughed. "They're also useless against us. Those shafts can't penetrate our uniforms."

"Then why would they use them?" Trant asked.

"For use against the San-Tarah," G'joth said impatiently. "They have no protection against them." *How did we get stuck with these imbeciles?* G'joth wondered. After almost a decade of serving with Davok on a variety of ships and squadrons, to find himself without his best friend was bad enough. True, he was an irritating, foolish malcontent of a *toDSaH*, but at least G'joth knew he could count on Davok to be there for him when it mattered. Trant and Maris had yet to earn such consideration. He'd fear for his own prospects for an honorable death if he didn't have such faith in Wol and Goran.

As for those archaic weapons, G'joth wasn't too concerned about them. Though that type of weapon was quite popular in the days before disruptors, it had fallen sufficiently out of favor with most warriors that G'joth couldn't even remember what it was called in Klingon. After all, if one wished to attack from a distance, one might as well use a disruptor, as it was infinitely more effective. As Wol pointed out, modern Klingon armor was proof against such bolts, and the weapon was useless for the more intimate combat provided by a knife or a sword.

In fact, G'joth was amazed that any such weapons even existed on the *K'mpec. Obviously, they have a collector on board.*

Trant then handed Wol a long-range viewer. Most of its settings were useless on this world, but its magnification capacity was mechanical, based on lenses, and so still had its uses. "Take a look at the bolts in those weapons."

Wol took the viewer and peered through it. "Those appear to be metallic."

"That's ridiculous," Maris said dismissively.

G'joth was less dismissive. He had assumed the shafts to be wooden.

Activating her communicator, Wol said, "Prepare grenade barrage." She then looked at Goran, G'joth, Trant, and Maris in turn. "We will focus our barrage on those with *QoSbows.* If those are metal shafts, they could do considerable damage to the three squads making the frontal assault, and they'll be taking heavy casualties as it is. Surprise is our best weapon right now."

"I still think this entire exercise is foolish."

G'joth finally lost his temper. "Then what are you

doing here, Trant? Does the call of battle not sing in your heart?"

"Of course it does!"

"Then *listen to it!* What does it matter if the foe is Klingon, Romulan, or Child of San-Tarah? What difference does it make who orders us to go into battle? What matters is that *we go into battle!* You are alongside fellow warriors, preparing to engage in that most pure of all pursuits! This is not a time to whine about motives like some kind of Ferengi. It is a time to celebrate!"

Goran, Maris, and some of the soldiers of the sixteenth who were nearby all murmured their approval of G'joth's words. Wol laughed and said, "You should have finished that poem, G'joth."

But G'joth thought only of Davok, who would never join him in battle again. He never missed his friend more than he did right now.

Wol, meanwhile, had put the viewer to her eyes again. "Something is wrong." She put the viewer down and activated her communicator a third time. "We are altering the plan. Fifteenth, Sixteenth, and Seventeenth Squads will engage in frontal assault. Eighteenth, Nineteenth, and Twentieth Squads, remain at your posts and prepare your grenades."

Maris scowled. "Why do we change the engagement at this late date?"

"Look at how the warriors armed with *QoSbows* are positioned," Wol said, handing Maris the viewer.

After several seconds staring at it, Maris said, "I see no pattern."

"Give me that," G'joth said angrily, snatching the viewer from Maris's hands. He looked, and saw that they were all positioned at intervals that seemed very specific. He had seen the pattern before, but could not place it.

Then, finally, he saw it. "The Battle of Kamross."

"Exactly," Wol said. "And they're positioned for an attack to the east."

Goran asked, "What is the Battle of Kamross?"

"A campaign fought by Kravokh before he ascended to the High Council," G'joth said. "He defended a valley similar to this by positioning warriors with disruptors to fend off a frontal assault at distant intervals so no one force could take all of them out from above."

Maris snarled. "So what? So we know that they will be ready for an assault. Only a fool would not be."

Wol turned to Maris. "They are ready for an assault *from the east*. They know our specific plan of attack. Which means there is a traitor in our midst. Therefore, I am changing the plan of attack. Are you questioning my orders, *Bekk?*"

Bowing his head, Maris said, "I would never do such a thing, Leader. I go where you command."

"Good. I command you now to prepare for a frontal assault. Our primary goal is to let them think they are being attacked from the south—then the other companies will begin the grenade barrage. Secondary goal is to locate the transporter blockers and capture them. Do *not* destroy them—we need to take them for our own use."

G'joth smiled. Even though Wol had gotten Davok and Krevor killed, they died with honor—she was a good Leader, and one he was proud to die for.

Wol raised her *mek'leth* above her head. "For Klag! For honor! For glory! For the Empire!"

"For the Empire!" G'joth and several others—though neither Maris nor Trant were among them—shouted back.

And the battle was joined.

The acrid smell of burning conduits brushed across Talak's nostrils as several of the *Akua*'s bridge consoles exploded. Fire control was handling the worst of it, keeping it from spreading around the bridge, but these damned rips in subspace were taking their toll on his ship.

His pilot screamed, "I still do not have helm control! We're drifting!"

Clenching his fist, Talak screamed right back. "Regain control *now!*"

The operations officer, in a much calmer tone, said, "Until we drift out of the eddy, sir, we cannot reliably use *any* control systems." Another console exploded, underlining her point.

"Find a way! I will not lose Klag now!" He unholstered his disruptor. "If this ship is not back under control in five minutes, you will pay for it with your life, Lieutenant!" He turned to the gunner, his disruptor still aimed at the operations officer's head. "Is there any way to fire weapons?"

The gunner shook his head. "Targeting systems are down. I can fire blindly, but I cannot guarantee that we will not hit an ally—or one of those mines."

"I have regained control!" the pilot said, even as the operations officer declared, "We have cleared the eddy."

Belatedly, Talak realized that his gesture had been an empty one. His hand weapon would no more fire within the subspace eddies than it would on the planet—or the ship's own disruptor cannons and arrays would. The tears in space rendered them useless. He had to hope that the operations officer either had forgotten, or was too concerned with her duties to notice. *I may have cost myself a great deal in the eyes of my crew.*

He stared at the viewer, which showed Klag's ship drifting, also a victim of this mad space. *You have done this to me. Like you have done so much to me and my House. But it ends today.*

"Firing control has returned," the gunner added, then looked at Talak and grinned. "I am locked on to the *Gorkon.*"

Talak returned the grin. "Arm four torpedoes and fire." To the pilot, he said, "Resume intercept course." Then he turned to the viewer, and watched as the four torpedoes headed toward the *Gorkon.* The Chancellor-class ship was drifting. *So much for your ability to map the eddies, Klag,* Talak thought with glee.

"Sir?"

Turning to the operations officer—who sounded unusually hesitant—Talak prompted, "Yes?"

"The sensors must be malfunctioning. I'm reading that the *Gorkon* is arming disruptors."

It took a moment for that to sink in. "What?"

"They're arming disruptors—and firing!"

Talak whirled back to the viewer just in time to see the *Gorkon's* disruptor array fire on and destroy all four of the *Akua's* torpedoes.

Damn him to Gre'thor, *he has outmaneuvered me* again! "You are a worthier foe than I imagined, Klag—that will only make your defeat and death sweeter. Arm a full spread of torpedoes! Fire on the *Gorkon!* And instruct Captain Huss to engage the *Gorkon* as well."

The gunner and operations officer acknowledged the order as one.

"Fire all disruptors!" Kornan cried, a huge grin on his face.

His bipolar feelings toward Kurak had firmly lodged in the wanting-to-ravage-her category. *I don't know what motivated you to find a way to make it work, but it may mean victory for us,* he thought at the chief engineer.

"Toq!" Klag bellowed from his chair to Kornan's left. "Switch to code *vagh* and pass on to our allies the modifications necessary to allow them to fire disruptors."

Kornan nodded. They had been using code *wej* up until now, but needed to switch to *vagh* now that Captain B'Edra had betrayed them.

"Sir," Toq said, "Commander Kurak's method may not work on other classes of ship."

Klag scowled, but Kornan quickly said, "They won't know that until have the opportunity to try, Lieutenant."

Toq grinned. "Good point. Altering code and sending now."

Kornan remembered the meeting in the wardroom days ago where they had discussed the codes. Klag had summoned Kornan, Lokor, and Toq to determine how best for the allies to communicate among each other. Using the Order of the *Bat'leth* frequency was immediately dismissed as impractical by the captain. "There may be Order inductees among Talak's fleet— we cannot afford to give them free intelligence."

Confidently, Toq said, "I can construct a code that will be intelligible only to those we give the key."

"Or any reasonably intelligent security officer," Lokor added. "We cannot count on it remaining unbroken for long."

Klag scratched his beard thoughtfully. "It will not need to be unbroken for long. Once the battle has begun, there will be precious little time for decoding. And only Talak's flagship—and Dorrek, if he comes—will have the personnel capable of such an action."

"Even if they do make the effort," Toq said, his

confident tone still evident, "they will first assume it to be a standard code and run through those before realizing it has nothing to do with them."

"You've created your own codes?" Kornan asked.

Suddenly Toq looked uncomfortable. "Let us say I have adapted a nonmilitary code for my own use."

"What do you mean?" Klag asked.

"I cannot say further, sir. Believe me when I tell you, though, that this code will not be broken under these circumstances."

Klag and Lokor exchanged a glance, and Lokor gave Klag a quick nod. *Lokor knows something about Toq that Klag does not,* Kornan had thought, *and that Toq may not even know that Lokor knows.* But then, that was Lokor's job as head of security.

"Very well, create the code."

Then Lokor asked, "Do you have more than one of these—nonmilitary codes that you can adapt, Lieutenant?"

"Several, why?"

Lokor looked at Klag. "There is a very strong possibility that some who answer your summons, Captain, may well side with General Talak—without informing you first."

"You fear treachery," Klag said.

"Fear? No. Expect, yes."

"Klingons betraying their honor," Toq said with disgust. "It is almost unthinkable."

Lokor snapped, "It is *very* thinkable, boy. Ideals are just that. In reality, we must account for the fact that not all Klingons are the noble creatures of honor we wish to be."

"One need not even be so cynical," Klag said, staring at an indeterminate point on the bulkhead. "I am sure that Talak sees his own actions as serving the cause of honor and his duty as a soldier of the Empire—as will those who follow him."

"Either way," Lokor said, "we will need to have more than one code in case such a betrayal occurs."

"What do you suggest?" Kornan asked.

"Create several codes. If and when allies do present themselves—"

"They will," Klag said.

Lokor fixed his captain with a look. "Your confidence is touching, sir, but I must be more realistic."

"Understood. Continue."

"We give them each all the codes, plus methods of decoding all but one of them—with each ship having a different one missing."

Klag nodded. "If one betrays us, we switch to the code that person cannot break."

"It is not perfect—if more than one of your fellow inductees chooses to betray us…"

"That will not happen," Klag said with confidence. "Induction into the Order is not something given lightly. I believe we can count on proper behavior from most of those chosen for such an honor. Moreover, anyone not inclined to support my call is far more likely to simply not show up."

Lokor smiled. "An excellent point."

Now Kornan thought back on that meeting, and came to two realizations. One was that Lokor was an invaluable asset to the *Gorkon.* The other was that Kornan himself need not have even shown up at the meeting for all that he contributed to it.

"Aft shields have not reconstituted!"

Grint's words brought Kornan back to the present and the battle they were engaged in. "Leskit, can you alter our heading to compensate for the lack of aft shields?"

"That depends."

"On?"

"How badly you wish to have the ship ripped to pieces by a subspace eddy."

Kornan cursed. His tactical display showed that the three birds-of-prey led by Captain Huss were on an intercept course with the *Gorkon*—they'd be in firing range in minutes.

Worse, the *Taj* destroyed the *Ch'marq,* leaving only the *Gorkon* and the *Vidd* among the original six still fighting and loyal to Klag. Obviously T'vis, B'Edra's first officer, did not feel that Klag's summons was the call to honor they'd hoped. *Or B'Edra overrode her first officer's wishes. Either way, we are losing valuable ground.*

"Sir," Kornan prompted.

"Not yet," Klag said. "It is best not to unholster all our weapons at once."

Kornan seethed, but said nothing.

"Torpedo bearing directly!" Toq said.

Then one of the secondary gunner positions ex-

ploded, just as a *bekk* took a seat at it. The station
had remained unstaffed, since those four positions at
the aft of the bridge controlled the four rotating disruptor arrays that, until a few moments ago, were in-
operative.

"Aft disruptor arrays five, six, and twelve offline!"
Toq said, even as Grint and the other *bekk* flew across
the bridge from the impact.

Kornan leapt from his station to the tactical post.
He saw the bodies of Grint and the other *bekk* on the
deck, bleeding profusely, but there was nothing to be
done for them now. If the opportunity presented itself, he would commend their souls to *Sto-Vo-Kor*; if
the opportunity didn't, then Kornan will have joined
them there.

Assuming that that is where I am bound . . .

He saw that Grint had programmed a standard firing pattern into the aft disruptors. *Foolish infant*, he
thought. *In this terrain, half the shots would go into the
eddies.* But Grint was not experienced—indeed, he
was only at that post because Rodek was injured and
Morketh was dead.

Not that it mattered, since the only aft disruptor
now working was the stationary one at the rearmost
part of the ship.

Kornan quickly programmed a new firing pattern
into the computer, making use of disruptor arrays ten
and eleven, which were better suited to targets closer
to the center of the ship's underside, but would have
to do in this case.

He checked the subspace eddies, then looked at the pilot's station. "Leskit, change course 182 mark 6!"

The pilot whirled around. "What?"

"Do it!"

To Kornan's annoyance, Leskit looked to Klag for confirmation; to the first officer's relief, Klag gave an instantaneous nod, and Leskit changed course.

Once the course change—which managed to keep them out of the eddies—was made, Kornan fired the aft disruptors, and ordered the *bekk* at one of the aft positions to fire arrays ten and eleven in the pattern he had laid out.

The *Akua*'s port wing, already badly damaged when it crashed into one of the eddies, exploded.

From his command chair, Klag pumped his fist in the air. "Well done, Kornan!"

Kornan grinned. *Perhaps I am bound for* Sto-Vo-Kor *after all. . . .*

"Sir!" Toq cried. Kornan looked over to see a look of glee on the second officer's face. "*K'Vort*-class vessel decloaking ten thousand *qell'qam*s off our port bow!"

Checking his own display, Kornan was able to verify the reading. "It's the *I.K.S. Kreltek*," he said, "under the command of Captain Triak." Then he looked up in fury. "They're hailing the *Akua!*"

CHAPTER EIGHT

Kalpok watched as fifteen warriors came charging down from the south, and thought that perhaps this would finally be the day he died.

I doubt I will be so lucky.

It had seemed such a good plan. Join the Defense Force as a soldier, get put into battle, die a heroic death, go to *Sto-Vo-Kor*. All his prospects for this life had been burned to ashes, so the best he could hope for was a proper entry into the next one. Suicide would send him straight to *Gre'thor*, and the circumstances that led to this sorry state of affairs meant that no one would give him *Mauk-to'Vor*.

That left combat. The best place to find that was the Defense Force, so he changed his name—identifying himself with his House was no longer prudent—and enlisted. He was assigned to one of the new Chancellor-class ships, the *K'mpec*, and figured he'd be dead inside a week.

No such luck. The *K'mpec* had had its share of battles, of course, and plenty of his comrades died gloriously, but Kalpok himself continued to breathe. He had been injured a few times, but nothing terribly serious—especially since Chancellor-class ships had medical facilities superior to those of other Defense Force vessels.

Now he stood in a valley on a primitive world in the Kavrot Sector hoping that the ground troops from another Defense Force vessel, the *Gorkon*, would do what none of the *K'mpec*'s other adversaries had managed.

One advantage: This was a much better place to die than Brenlek had been. The *K'mpec*'s last assignment was to begin the process of conquering that world. A barely post-industrial society populated by hairless bipeds with gray skin and wide black eyes, Brenlek was foul-smelling, with smoke choking the air and filth on the ground. It was like swimming in a cesspool. The Brenlekki fought poorly; they had numbers on their side, and some powerful explosive weapons, which only meant it took an extra day or two to fully conquer them. Kalpok had killed several dozen of them himself. But they were no challenge, and there was little glory to be gained in dying on so foul a planet. Even the Brenlekki blood—of which Kalpok had spilled a fair quantity—had a wretched stench. The blood of one's foes should roar in one's nostrils, but the blue Brenlekki blood smelled like industrial waste, just like their world.

It was a bad place to die.

San-Tarah, however, was a worthy place to give one's life. This world's scents were all of trees and grass and wildlife.

And blood, the smell of which made any warrior's heart sing with joy in spilling it. That came later, of course.

The natives of this world were far worthier opponents. Kalpok was as likely to die from accidentally falling into one of the waste-extractor-like rivers on Brenlek than from actual combat. More Brenlekki surrendered to him than fought him; if the so-called Children of San-Tarah had a concept of surrender, no one in this village subscribed to it. These were worthy foes who fought to the bitter end.

I cannot believe my life has led to this.

Kalpok was born to a noble and successful House, the son of Nakob, the owner of one of the finest weapons-makers in the Empire. Or, at least, that's what he thought, until the party following his reaching the Age of Ascension. Then, Nakob—who was, at that point, quite drunk—informed him that his parents were Nakob's cousin Eral and some lowborn dalliance of hers. Kalpok's father had been put to death, Eral exiled, and Kalpok given to Nakob to raise. "And you've done me proud, boy, you truly have!" was the last thing Nakob said before he passed out.

Nakob never brought the subject up again, and

Kalpok was perfectly happy to let it go—right up until eight months ago. Their House had supported the traitor Morjod in his attempt to wrest control of the Empire from Chancellor Martok. When Martok triumphed, Kalpok's House was disgraced. He didn't even dare think the House's name now, for it was not to be mentioned.

Strictly speaking, Kalpok should have died with the rest of his family. But when Martok retook the chancellor's seat and had the Great Hall rebuilt, Kalpok managed to avoid the vengeance. For the first time since reaching the Age of Ascension, he acknowledged the words that Nakob had drunkenly imparted to him.

My parents were not part of our House—my mother was cast out, and my father was never part of it in the first place. So I should not be held accountable for their actions.

Of course, he still was left with nowhere to go, nothing to do—except die well. That was the true wish of every Klingon, to die a glorious death and ascend to *Sto-Vo-Kor*. Kalpok hadn't been entirely sure that was his true wish for most of his life—but the actions of his family in supporting a lunatic's attempted coup left him with few options. It was either go for the good death or settle for the miserable life ending in a bad death.

Besides, the Defense Force provides regular meals. Before hatching this particular plan, he had spent the better part of a week living on the streets of the Old Quarter of the First City. He had no desire to relive *that* experience ever again, not after living in the lap of House Varnak's luxury for so long....

He cursed. *Don't think the name. They are not your House. That House does not exist. Neither do you. You are Bekk Kalpok—no House, no known father, just a soldier of the Empire. One of those fifteen Klingons heading toward you right now is going to run his or her d'k tahg through your heart, you will die a painful and glorious death, and this will finally be over.*

Kalpok was a bit confused at the attack, though. They had been told to expect the frontal assault to come from the south. Someone on the *Gorkon* was apparently feeding information to the *K'mpec's QaS DevwI'*, and that intelligence indicated a southern assault.

Not that Kalpok cared all that much. He wasn't even sure what this fight was all about, or why they were fighting other Klingons along with these furry natives. All he knew was that Leader Tann ordered him to fight, and so he fought, and would continue to fight until he finally got to die.

The next thing he knew, he was prone on the ground, a ringing in his ears so loud it threatened to blow his head wide open.

After a moment, he realized that he'd been knocked to the ground by an explosion. *How is that possible? The QaS DevwI' told us that energy weapons wouldn't work here!* They hadn't even been issued hand disruptors.

Another explosion followed, farther away. Then a third. The noise filled his very bones, his heart slamming against his rib cage, which seemed to vibrate with the endless, all-encompassing *noise*. Even with the sounds of combat, San-Tarah had been pastoral and *quiet* until these be-damned explosions.

Kalpok struggled to get to his feet. His knees wobbled, but he somehow managed to steady himself upright. *Where did those explosions come from?*

Around him were the sights of battle. The sounds were probably there, too, but Kalpok did not hear them—his ears still rang with the after-effects of the explosions so loudly that the noise seemed to burrow through his ears and into his brain.

He unsheathed his *tik'leth* as a Klingon woman ran toward him, wielding a *bat'leth*. Kalpok hated *bat'leth*s. They were too complicated. So many different maneuvers and holds and grips—he spent so much time trying to figure out how to handle the damned thing he couldn't fight properly with it. The *tik'leth* was basic—the pointed end went into the opponent. Much simpler.

The Klingon swung down her *bat'leth*, which Kalpok parried fairly easily. They traded cuts for several minutes before Kalpok found an opening in the woman's left side. He thrust his *tik'leth* into her flank, the tip of the blade rending her armor and tasting her blood.

She took a swing in response, but it was weak, and Kalpok dodged it fairly easily. Before she died, she said something, but Kalpok still couldn't hear a thing. Not that he cared what so unworthy an opponent had to say.

Pulling out his *tik'leth* and kicking the woman's body to the ground, Kalpok looked around for a fresh opponent. Smoke filled the air, and some kind of chemical stench mixed with the blood and plant life. Suddenly, Kalpok felt as though he were back on Brenlek. *The explosives—they must be chemical in nature.* Kalpok did not enjoy the realization; it was taking the luster off his glorious death.

But the smoke combined with the ringing in his ears meant he couldn't really tell what was going on. So he stood and waited for a foe to come to him. *If I'm lucky, it'll be someone more talented than this woman and I'll finally get to* Sto-Vo-Kor.

He never saw the *mek'leth* that slammed into his back.

Whirling around, he swung his *tik'leth*, hoping to at least put up a fight. It collided with the gauntlet of another woman, this one with auburn hair, who had raised her left arm to block his attack.

He took another swing. The *mek'leth* was still in his back, and he could feel the life pouring out of him, but now he had an unarmed foe to face—if he was going to die, this was the way to do it, bringing down the enemy with him.

Then he got a good look at the woman he faced. Her auburn tresses framed a battle-hardened face—

—and a crest identical to Kalpok's own.

By the hand of Kahless, no.

"E—Eral?"

Kalpok could not actually hear himself say the words, but apparently the woman who might well be his mother could, as she stopped moving, her jaw hanging open. She had been about to unsheathe her *d'k tahg* to finish what the *mek'leth* started. Now, though, she just stared.

Unfortunately, Kalpok had no idea what she said next. Nor could he focus, as the smoke was irritating his eyes, and his knees started to wobble again.

I don't believe this, he thought as he collapsed to the ground, suddenly unable to feel his legs at all. The ground collided with his head, dirt entering his mouth and eyes. He barely noticed. *I may have finally found my mother, and she's the one who kills me.*

On the other hand, he mused as the blackness overtook him, *it seems only fitting.*

Dorrek clenched his fist and slammed it onto the arm of his chair in frustration. Nothing was going according to plan. His ground troops were being overrun by Klag's own troops as well as those be-snouted native creatures, and they had lost four ships.

At least we now have the Taj. Talak had indicated that they might get assistance, but had not said from whom. Having the *K'Vort*-class vessel fighting on the side of right would prove beneficial, both in terms of evening the fight in orbit and in the additional troops the ship could provide on San-Tarah.

Still and all, it would have been better if they'd shown

their true colors sooner. They only really held two villages on the planet, and the latest reports from the *QaS DevwI'* indicated that they were losing ground in Val-Goral thanks to the use of explosives.

Dorrek shook his head. *Explosives. Of course.* He had let his hatred for his older brother blind him to the fact that Klag had always been resourceful. For someone who always carried on about "the way of things," he had a remarkable ability to make the best of bad situations.

Though Klag was a year older, they both went to officer training at the same time. At one point, they and others of their unit were brought to Rura Penthe. The frozen planet was primarily home to the Empire's largest prison, but the bulk of the world's surface area was unused. Each warrior was dropped into the middle of a wide expanse of ice without food or weapons and told to walk to the Defense Force outpost at the planet's north pole. They were not told how far they had to go, or which direction north was, or what obstacles would be in their path (beyond the obvious one of the frigid temperatures). Some of the local fauna might attack a lone, defenseless warrior— though it was nothing that even an unarmed Klingon shouldn't have been able to handle, and any who couldn't were quickly killed and weeded out of the officer corps. Others were similarly weeded by proceeding in a direction other than north.

As one grew closer to the pole, there was a patch of ice that was far too thin to support a person's weight. That, in fact, was the point at which most ended their test, for the patch was six hours away from the beam-down point, and any who made it that far were unable to survive being dropped into the frigid water underneath the ice, and were beamed out and allowed to heal. Indeed, that was how far Dorrek went, after fighting off two small ursine bipeds and a winged monstrosity, and barely escaping an avalanche.

The point of the test, Dorrek would later understand, was to see how far each warrior got. No one had ever successfully made it to the Defense Force outpost, mainly because no such outpost existed on Rura Penthe. The warriors were rated on how far they got before succumbing, by how long they continued to fight for their lives.

Klag, however, received the top ranking in their class by virtue of making it almost to the pole. He not only survived all the planet's hardships, but thrived in them. Though battered, frozen, and exhausted, he realized the ice would not support his weight before he fell through it. So he fashioned a raft from some of the thicker ice, and used two icicle shards as bladed weapons that he could wield to clear a path through the water, enabling his raft to sail through before it had a chance to freeze back over.

Those efforts took their toll, of course, and Klag collapsed in the snow shortly after making that last journey past the thin ice.

Most warriors who did well claimed shame at not

completing their mission afterward, only to be assured by the trainers that they did exactly what they were supposed to do and that there was no dishonor in their performance.

Klag, however, managed to scrape together his strength and demand that he be returned to the surface to complete his task, that he had been disgraced, not by his own collapse, but by being beamed out before he was finished. Looking back, Dorrek mused that it not only set the tone for Klag's determination, but also for his insistence on blaming others for his own failures—the trainers, M'Raq, Kargan, Dorrek himself...

Now, Dorrek thought, *he has managed to construct another raft to sail through the deadly waters.* Having succeeded in mining the subspace eddies and figuring out how to fire disruptors, he also brought explosives to a world where energy weapons did not work.

"Contact engineering," he said to his operations officer, "and tell them that, if they cannot determine how to fire disruptors within the hour, I will have them all killed and replaced with the maintenance staff."

"Yes, sir."

Klag, of course, finished ahead of Dorrek at officer training. He was promoted faster than Dorrek—until the *Pagh*, when Klag found himself serving as a commander for almost ten years, first officer of General Talak's Housemate Kargan.

And never seeing our father until after he died, and then only to befoul his shell. Klag should have been leading their House to glory, but he had abdicated that right long ago.

"Tactical display."

He viewed the field of battle on the main viewer. Captain Huss's three ships were threading their way through the eddies toward where the *Gorkon* faced off against the now-crippled *Akua.* The *Taj* and the *Gogam* had taken up position with the *K'mpec* in orbit. The *Vidd* was off sensors, probably hiding in the eddies.

"Tell the *Taj* and the *Gogam* to seek out and destroy the *Vidd.* We will aid—"

"Sir," the operations officer interrupted, "a *K'Vort*-class ship is decloaking fifteen thousand *qell'qams* off the *Akua's* starboard bow." She looked up. "It's the *Kreltek,* sir."

Whose side are they on? Dorrek wondered, then realized that there was only one answer. "My brother has received new blood." He thought a moment. Three birds-of-prey and a damaged *Vor'cha* would be sufficient against just Klag, but adding the *Kreltek* to the mix would give his brother an advantage that Dorrek saw no reason to provide.

"Pilot, plot a course to the *Gorkon.*"

"Sir, we cannot."

Dorrek snarled. "What!?"

The pilot, an old man whom Dorrek knew had seen more campaigns than Dorrek had seen years, turned around, a defiant expression on his face. "There is no direct course to the *Gorkon's* position that is not blocked by the subspace eddies or one of the six ships."

"Then take an indirect course, but *do it*."

"Yes, sir," the pilot said.

Unsurprisingly, Dorrek saw the *Kreltek* fire on the *Akua*. *Definitely one of Klag's fellow members of the Order, damn them*.

"Sir, those torpedoes are inert," the operations officer said.

Dorrek grinned. "Obviously, my brother has not had the opportunity to brief his allies on how to modify their weapons."

The operations officer wasn't finished, however. "Sir, the *Jor* is firing—disruptors!"

Whirling around to the operations station, Dorrek cried, "What!?"

"Disruptors, sir—at half power."

Turning back to the viewer, Dorrek watched as Captain Huss's lead ship's disruptor cannons fired toward the *Akua*.

This is wrong. If Captain Huss has determined how to fire disruptors, why has she not shared this intelligence?

Then his eyes widened as he realized that they were *not* heading for the *Akua*, but two of the inert photon torpedoes that the *Kreltek* had fired. *Good*, Dorrek thought, *she is destroying the torpedoes before they strike the* Akua. Even inert, the torpedoes could still do physical damage, especially to the unshielded and damaged portions of the *Akua*'s port side, like the gaping hole where its wing used to be.

But wait—why half power?

The disruptors struck the torpedoes—

—and detonated them!

Dorrek leapt to his feet, letting out a snarl of rage. "Pilot, when will we—?"

The pilot didn't even wait for him to finish. "Fifteen minutes at this speed. If we go any faster," he added before Dorrek could tell him to increase it, "we risk entry into the—"

"I don't give a *damn* what we risk! Full impulse! I want to destroy that traitor myself!"

It is not enough that you disgrace me and our House, Klag, but now you bring down a great warrior like Huss. Dorrek had always admired Huss and was, in fact, gratified when Talak told him that she would be joining the fleet instead of Worvag's trio of ships. Her strikes against the Dominion as part of Talak's fleet were the stuff of song, and Dorrek had been honored to be fighting alongside her.

Now, though, he understood why Huss had requested the change—*so she could stab us in the back.* He supposed that Huss was part of the Order—he had never paid especial attention to their rolls—and that accounted for her betrayal now. *It will be the last thing she does, if I have anything to say about it.*

"Has engineering determined a way to fire disruptors yet?" Dorrek asked.

"Not yet, sir."

Of course not. "Arm photon torpedoes, prepare to fire them as soon as the *Jor* is in range!"

He turned back to the viewer. The *Akua* was turning about, retreating, even as the *Gorkon*, *Kreltek*, and Huss's ships gave chase; Talak was firing multiple shots on the enemy, of course, forcing them to keep their distance.

"In range," the operations officer said.

That was quick. Giving a nod of approval to the pilot for getting them to the site of battle without hitting any of the eddies, Dorrek then said, "Fire on the *Jor!*"

"We're being targeted by the *Kreltek!*"

"Ignore them." Dorrek was not about to be distracted. "Continuous fire."

Suddenly, half the alarms on the bridge went off, and most of the lights. Damage reports were shouted over each other—the structural-integrity field, shields, weapons, helm control, all were offline.

The pilot said, "We've hit one of the *Gorkon*'s mines, sir—and one of the eddies! All systems are down—we're drifting!"

Dorrek clenched his fist and slammed it onto the arm of his chair in frustration.

As Goran killed his fifth Klingon since the attack on Val-Goral bagan, he decided that he was glad that G'joth and Leader Wol had talked him out of *Mauk-to'Vor*.

In an entire life of being the biggest and the strongest, Goran had never lost a fight, whether during his days as a prison guard on Rura Penthe or as a soldier in the Defense Force. Then he had engaged in the contest of strength against the Children of San-Tarah and lost. A native named Fe-Ruv held a koltanium rock on her back for a full four hundred seconds longer than Gorn had.

Losing was a feeling he did not appreciate, nor did he know if he could live with it. However, Wol and G'joth—the only survivors of his squad—convinced him to go on living.

Now he was glad he did. They had charged down the hill the way Leader Wol had asked, and now were killing their enemies. Goran didn't say anything, but he was glad that Wol had changed the plan. Originally, the fifteenth was supposed to remain on top of the incline and throw grenades, but Goran didn't see the point in that. As big and strong as he was—even if he wasn't actually biggest and strongest anymore—it seemed silly for him to just throw grenades. *Anybody* could do that.

He said nothing, of course, because he obeyed Leader Wol. She was a good Leader, and Goran thought it was a great honor to serve under her.

Instead, though, Wol changed the plan at the last minute so that the other squads threw the grenades and they got to attack in person.

If anyone asked him, Goran would not have been able to explain why it was that they were fighting other Klingons. Wol had said that they were dishonoring the captain, which was all Goran needed to know. Captain Klag was his commander. If he had been dishonored, then Goran would do everything he could to fight back to restore that honor.

Coughing a few times from the smoke in the air that the grenades caused, Goran sliced through three more Klingons with one swipe of his *bat'leth*, then grabbed a fourth by the head and snapped her neck. Then he turned and looked around.

He could not see any other members of his squad, or of the sixteenth or seventeenth. However, he did see almost a dozen Klingons surrounding him, each holding either *bat'leths* or *mek'leths*. Or maybe it was over a dozen; Goran had always had trouble counting, especially in the heat of battle.

"You will not take this city from us, *toDSaH*," one of them said as he twirled his *bat'leth* in a traditional preparatory gesture. Goran noticed that he had the medallion of a squad leader on his right biceps. "And once we kill you, we will eliminate the rest of your dishonorable crew."

Goran said nothing. He never understood why anyone would talk in the middle of a battle. In fact, Goran rarely had anything to say even when he wasn't fighting, and when he was, he had other things to worry about than making conversation.

All of the Klingons ran toward him at once. For a moment, Goran wasn't sure what to do—who did he defend against first when so many came at once from all sides?

Several bodies collided with his hip and legs. Even as he blocked a *bat'leth* swipe with his own *bat'leth*, another one slammed into his left arm. He let out a kick that knocked two of them aside, but the blade of a *d'k tahg* sliced into his right hand, almost forcing him to drop his *bat'leth*. One Klingon leapt up onto his back and tried to choke him. Goran couldn't do anything about that, so he ignored him, hoping that his hands would get free before the one on his back choked all the air out of him.

More bodies collided with him, trying to tackle him about the waist. Goran quickly lost count of how many he'd knocked off him or of how many were currently trying to kill him—not that it mattered. What mattered was that there were too many.

Both his arms were now pinned, he had dropped his *bat'leth*, and it was getting harder to breathe, though he wasn't sure how much of that was because of the smoke from the grenades or the Klingon who was trying to choke him. The smoke was definitely starting to irritate his eyes. He kicked with one leg, hoping it would dislodge someone. The sound of bone snapping came a moment later, but Goran didn't notice any change in the number of Klingons on top of him. *For warriors who dishonored Captain Klag, they do fight well.* Usually breaking a bone meant that a warrior would at least pause in battle or have a mild setback. But these hung on.

Something struck Goran's legs, and he lost his ability to stay upright. Letting out a scream of annoyance, he fell backward.

Now they piled on top of him. The only benefit

from falling down was that the pressure on his neck ceased. Goran figured that the one on his back was crushed by Goran's own weight. He had done that a few times at Rura Penthe—restrained prisoners by the simple expedient of sitting on them.

Unfortunately, now he felt the cut of multiple blades slicing through his armor. He tried to shove the Klingons off him, and managed to get two or three to stop stabbing him, but that still left several more.

Then, suddenly, many Klingons were thrown off of him by some outside force. Goran looked up to see a massive Child of San-Tarah holding one Klingon in each of her paws while kicking two more. She then threw the two aside and drew her weapon, the curved, two-bladed weapon that they used.

Goran recognized his rescuer. It was Fe-Ruv, the one who had defeated him.

With several of his foes removed by Fe-Ruv, Goran was able to throw the remainder—who were distracted by the surprise of Fe-Ruv's attack—off him and get up again. When he did, Goran noted that the one who had jumped on his back still lay on the ground, his chest and head crushed.

"I am told," Fe-Ruv said, "that your people do not like to ask for assistance. But you looked like you needed help, and I thought together we could show these—what is your word? *pa-tak?*—what it means to be strong."

The Leader, whose left arm was hanging uselessly from his shoulder and was bleeding from a wound in his cheek, growled. "You would hide behind this creature, *Bekk?*"

"I'm not hiding from anyone!" Goran said. "And I'm not the one who has to lead over a dozen warriors so I can lose to one Klingon." Then he smiled. "Or to one Klingon and one San-Tarah." He looked at Fe-Ruv. "Let's show them."

The Leader raised his *bat'leth*. "Kill them!"

Without even having to communicate to each other, Goran and Fe-Ruv stood back to back, Fe-Ruv holding her sword. *It is like we were meant to do this,* Goran thought.

Then the few Klingons still left attacked.

Goran punched one in the face, driving the bones of his nose into his brain, killing him immediately. Another swung her *mek'leth* at Goran, which he blocked with a gauntlet, then grabbed her neck with his other hand and crushed her throat. Tossing her aside, he then took a swing with his fist at two more, downing them with a single blow that resulted in spurting blood and flying teeth.

From behind him, Goran heard more cries of pain, and also saw spurts of Klingon blood, probably the work of Fe-Ruv's sword. Goran had lost his *bat'leth* somewhere along the line. He supposed he could have taken a moment to pick it up—or one of the many other weapons that had been dropped along with their wielders—but Goran was enjoying simply bashing his foes. Maybe he wasn't the biggest and the strongest, but he and Fe-Ruv were the *two* biggest and strongest—and like the Child of San-Tarah said, this was their chance to show them what that meant.

A few minutes later, they were surrounded by bleeding and broken Klingon corpses—except for the Leader, who was now holding a *d'k tahg* with his right hand.

"You are a fool," the Leader said to Goran. "You obey the orders of a fool, and you ally yourself with inferiors."

Goran walked up to the Leader, who did not back away even as Goran loomed over him. "You're the only inferior I see here."

Then he hit the Leader very hard on the top of his head with a closed fist. The Leader fell to the ground, his *d'k tahg* clattering to the ground next to him on top of a discarded *tik'leth*.

Fe-Ruv's tongue was hanging outside her mouth, just as it had been after she had been holding the rock for several hours. Unlike that time, her fur was matted down with Klingon blood. It gave her a nice smell, though it was hard for Goran to pick up the scent, as the air was still choked with those grenades that G'joth made. Her sword was also covered in blood.

"We make a good team, you and I, Goran."

"Yes, we do. We are the biggest and the strongest."

She then reared her head back and howled.

Several other howls came in response.

The day had been won.

So what if he wasn't biggest and the strongest anymore? Goran was still plenty big and strong enough to serve his captain and the Empire. That was all that mattered to him.

The faces of two women looked at Klag from the viewer of his bridge. The one on the left had been his secret weapon, the *d'k tahg* he'd hidden in his boot in order to slice Talak's throat when he least expected it: Huss, who had answered Klag's call in secret, remaining inside Talak's fleet until the best opportunity presented itself. Just as the *Taj* had turned against Klag, now he had turned the *Jor*, *Nukmay*, and *Khich* on Talak.

The one on the right was a face he had not expected to see, and hadn't laid eyes on since his days on the *Pagh*: Vekma, who was apparently now the *Kreltek*'s captain. Klag had had Toq send the *Kreltek* code *vagh* and its decoding procedure.

"*Captain Triak had to be replaced when he refused to do his duty as requested by a member of the Order of the* Bat'leth," Vekma said.

"You're in the Order?" Klag asked.

"*No, but my new first officer is.*" Vekma smiled that toothy smile that Klag remembered quite fondly from the old days on the *Pagh*. "*Hevna was insistent that we respond to your call to battle. When Triak was unwilling to do so, I took action.*" She laughed, a musical sound. "*To be honest, Klag, I'm grateful. Fawning over that arrogant petaQ was getting to be a chore. And he was dreadful in bed.*"

Klag threw his head back and laughed. Vekma was an adventurous lover. She and Klag had shared a bed more than once before she transferred to another post. For that matter, Klag recalled that she was the one who expressed curiosity as to how Klag's friend and comrade William Riker—a human Starfleet officer serving a brief tour as the *Pagh*'s first officer over a decade ago—would perform.

Huss did not share the laugh. She stared at Klag with sharp green eyes that complemented her flame red hair. *"What are your orders, Captain?"*

"I would not ask you to fire on your commander again. Take your ships and pursue the *Taj* and the *Gogam*. Attempt to herd them toward the remaining mines. Vekma, you and I will take the *Akua*."

"What of the K'mpec?" Huss asked.

Klag turned to Toq. "Any change in readings?"

"No, sir. The *K'mpec* is dead in space."

Turning back to the viewer, Klag said, "Leave them. If they regain power, we will deal with them, then."

"Sentiment will prove our undoing, Captain. I am perfectly content to fire on Talak if I must—in fact, I already have. You cannot afford to—"

"Do not presume to tell me what I may or may not do with regards to my brother, Captain Huss!" Klag snapped. "You have your orders! If you will not follow them, then return your flag to General Talak's command."

"I follow the course of honor, Captain Klag," Huss said tightly. *"When I contacted you two days ago, I*

swore fealty to you in this cause, as befits a member of the Order. You gave your word to the Children of San-Tarah. I will not besmirch that because I find your strategy lacking. Out."

Her face disappeared from the viewer, leaving only Vekma. "*We've both come a long way, haven't we, Klag?*"

Now Klag allowed himself a smile. "Not really. Ten years ago, we struggled for honor despite having a fool for a commander. Today is no different—only it is Talak who is the fool instead of Kargan."

"*Perhaps we should just eliminate the entire House of K'Tal and have done with it.*"

"One step at a time." Klag grinned. "*Qapla'*, Vekma!"

"*Qapla', Klag.*"

The viewer returned to the spacescape. From behind Klag, Kornan said, "Leskit, plot a course toward the *Akua*, and execute at full impulse."

"Weapons?" Klag asked.

"Forward disruptors armed and ready, sir," Kornan said.

"*Kreltek* taking up position forty thousand *qell'qams* to starboard," Leskit said. Then he whirled around. "Sir, they're on course to hit one of the mines!"

"Toq—" Klag started.

"I am alerting Captain Vekma, sir," Toq said calmly.

"In range of *Akua*," Kornan said, then quickly added, "They are changing course."

"Keep with them, Leskit, and fire when ready, Kornan."

"Sir!" Toq cried. "I'm reading an instability in the *Akua*'s warp core!"

Klag rose from his chair, ignoring the fact that he listed to his right. "Verify!"

As Toq checked his readings, Leskit said, "Captain, I just noticed something you *really* aren't going to like."

Turning to the old pilot, Klag prompted, "What?"

"The *Akua*'s course change puts us directly in the path of their warp-core ejection systems."

"Verified, sir—*Akua* warp core will explode in twenty-eight seconds," Toq said.

"Evasive maneuvers! Alert the *Kreltek* as well—will any of the other ships be in range?"

"No, sir," Toq said, "but—" He hesitated.

Klag suddenly knew why. One of the ways to combat a subspace weapon was to seal the subspace rip caused by such a device with a warp core. Klag recalled that Riker had used just such a technique over a year ago on the *Enterprise*.

The question was, what effect would this warp core have on the subspace eddies?

"They're ejecting the core," Toq said.

Leskit added, "And it's heading straight for us."

CHAPTER NINE

Wol stared down in disbelief at the corpse lying at her feet, her *mek'leth* lodged in his back.

No. It cannot be. It simply cannot.

But it was. She could feel it in her very bones, in her *heart*, that the boy whom she had just killed—whom she had stabbed *in the back*—was her son. Never mind that she hadn't seen him since shortly after giving birth, since her father took the child away from her before casting her out of the House of Varnak. He had her crest. He had her eyes. He looked to be the right age.

And she just killed him.

Or perhaps not.

Several howls cut through the ever-diminishing sounds of battle—first one, followed by several more. Over the past week, Wol had come to recognize the different howls of the Children of San-Tarah. This one was the cry of victory. Soon, the howls were joined by Klingons screaming their own cries of victory, and a few breaking into song.

Even as conflicting strains of both the Warrior's Anthem and "Don't Speak" wafted through the air in a variety of keys, Wol activated her communicator. "Wol to Goran—report to my position immediately."

"I am coming, Leader Wol."

She looked around, but she could barely see a thing with all the smoke in the air from G'joth's grenades. Not that she was complaining. They had retaken Val-Goral, thanks mainly to the surprise of the grenades.

"Ch'drak to Wol."

That was the Leader of the sixteenth. Wol had last seen him leading both his squad and the seventeenth to the command post that the *K'mpec's QaS Devwl'* had set up at the center of the village. With irritation at the interruption, she activated her communicator. "What?"

"We have secured the transporter blockers."

Wol shook her head. *The battle. You are Leader, do not lose sight of the battle.*

Goran came lumbering up to Wol, alongside G'joth. "You sent for me, Leader?"

"Well done, Ch'drak," Wol said, gesturing for Goran to wait. "Deactivate the blockers and beam them to the *Gorkon*."

"The Gorkon *is not in transporter range right now, Leader."*

Frowning, Wol started to say something; then a

thought occurred. "Bring them to me, then. *Bekk* Goran and I will be returning to the Prime Village. You are to remain in charge until you hear otherwise from the *QaS DevwI'*, Ch'drak."

"*As you say, Leader.*"

"Out." Wol didn't like the tone of voice Ch'drak used—it sounded like he thought she was showing weakness. *Well, let him think that. I have other concerns.*

She looked at the two *bekks*. For the first time, she noticed that Goran's uniform was covered with tears in the leather and rents in the armor, and also smeared on the outside with blood. The big man himself had no obvious cuts or bruises, though. *Typical,* Wol thought with some small amusement. "You've been busy, Goran."

"Yes, Leader," Goran said proudly. "Fe-Ruv and I demolished three squads." Then he frowned. "I think it was three squads. There were a lot, anyhow."

"Well done, Goran. Now, I need you to pick up that body. We will be bringing it to B'Oraq's *HoSpI'tal,* see if he can be saved."

Even as Goran moved to follow her order, G'joth stared at her. "What are you doing, Leader?"

"This is not your concern, G'joth."

"Leader, *you* are responsible for this campaign. And we have won it, but don't forget that we have a traitor in our midst. You cannot just leave us in the hands of Ch'drak—what if *he* is the traitor?"

Wol scowled at G'joth. Her first instinct was to kill him for his insolence, but insolence was a large part of what made G'joth who he was. Besides which, he was right. She was letting her personal life interfere with duty.

Yet how can I not?

"Goran," she said after a moment, "you will bring this soldier and the blockers back to the Prime Village." He was probably the only person who could physically handle both. "Bring the soldier to B'Oraq and tell her to do everything she can to keep him alive."

"What's so important—" G'joth started.

"Are you questioning my orders, *Bekk?*"

G'joth started. In their time on the *Gorkon*, Wol had not had the need to take this particular tone with any of her squad. They had become a tight fighting unit without the need for her to enforce her rank.

"Of course not, Leader."

"Good." She was still left with a conundrum, as she had already given Ch'drak command. Now she had a choice between taking it back and weakening her own position or standing by her orders and leaving the mission vulnerable to a saboteur.

The mission must take precedence.

"Wol to Vok," she said, activating her communicator.

"*Vok.*"

"We have taken Val-Goral."

"*Excellent!*"

"*Bekk* Goran will be bringing the transporter

blockers—as well as a prisoner to be taken to Dr. B'Oraq." She hesitated. "I will be escorting the prisoner."

"Why?"

Wol chose her words carefully. "The troops stationed here were prepared for our attack. However, we were able to discern that beforehand, and so changed the attack. It is why we were victorious. This prisoner may know who the traitor is in our midst."

"Have Goran bring the prisoner back, but I want you to stay there, Leader. Make sure the village remains secure and try to ascertain who the traitor is. I'd rather just be able to kill the prisoner."

"Yes, sir." Wol let out a long breath.

She then contacted the Leader of Sixteenth Squad. "Ch'drak, there has been a change. *QaS DevwI'* Vok has instructed me to remain here. *Bekk* Goran will bring the blockers to the Prime Village."

"Very well." Ch'drak didn't sound pleased.

G'joth stared at Wol. "What would you have done if Vok hadn't provided you with an easy way to sidestep your honor?"

"I have my reasons, G'joth. Do not question me again."

Putting up a hand, G'joth said, "As the Leader commands." Then he grinned. "But at least you could have given my grenades *some* credit for our victory to Vok."

Wol laughed. "It will be in my official report,

worry not, G'joth." She turned to Goran. "Go on, *Bekk*, get back to the Prime Village immediately."

"You can count on me, Leader."

Nurse Gaj checked on her patient. If the *bolmaq* had been present, this would have been a tedious process involving examination of scanning data, possibly the application of whatever arcane chemicals the patient might require, or tending to the patient's need in some manner or other. The *bolmaq*—which was how Gaj mentally referred to B'Oraq—could be tiresome that way. Gaj had coined the name shortly after reporting to the *Gorkon* on Qo'noS seven months ago. A *bolmaq* was a small, furry animal from Boreth that had a high-pitched bleat that it uttered whenever it ran around in circles, something it was compelled to do at random intervals. It was similar to the *Gorkon's* doctor in both nomenclature and, as far as Gaj was concerned, temperament.

With the *bolmaq* currently on the planet performing her obscene sorceries on the ground troops and the alien filth of that world, Gaj limited her activities to making sure that the medical bay's lone patient—Lieutenant Rodek—was still alive.

The biobed gave readings indicating that Rodek still drew breath.

Satisfied, Gaj sat down with her padd and started reading *Burning Hearts of Qo'noS*. It had been weeks since she read it last. She decided to skip ahead to Ngara's duel with Lughor—that was always her favorite part, and it meant she wouldn't have slog through all the buildup. *Sometimes I wonder why authors waste time like this. I just want to get to the good part.*

Certainly reading this romance was more exciting than anything that went on in her life. The songs told of glorious battles that warriors fought, but after seven months on an allegedly top-of-the-line Klingon Defense Force vessel, Gaj decided that there was a thing or two she could tell those songwriters. "Glorious battle" was a myth. All it was was shouting and blood, and it was exceedingly boring.

Serving in this nightmare of a medical bay made it all the worse. By going into nursing and joining the Defense Force, she thought she had assured herself of a career that would involve little work and maximum exposure to the heroes of the Empire. After all, what work would there be, truly, beyond the bandaging of the occasional wound, the severing of the occasional limb, the fitting of the occasional eyepatch.

But no, she had to be stuck with a revolutionary. The *bolmaq* wanted to change the face of Klingon medicine, to improve the lot of warriors' lives by healing them.

It was stupid. Did Lughor need radical medical procedures after Ngara wounded him? Of course not. He was a warrior consumed by passion, unconcerned with trivialities like injuries.

Gaj could not wait for this mission to Kavrot to be over. By then, her term would be up and she could go elsewhere. Anything to get away from the *bolmaq* and her insanity.

The worst was when she had to help the *bolmaq* graft an arm onto the captain. It had been all Gaj could do to keep from emptying the contents of both her stomachs on the operating table. When Ngara cut off B'Entra's arm in the opening fight in *Burning Hearts*, B'Entra did not go to some Federation-trained *petaQ* and have a new arm attached so she could exact her revenge. No, she plotted her revenge in much more clever ways, paving the way for the climactic duel between them on the mountains overlooking Lughor's estate. To do otherwise would have no poetry.

But the *bolmaq*, Gaj had learned, had no poetry, either.

Gaj had allowed herself some hope a few months ago when the *bolmaq* had gone off with some human doctor in the captain's personal transport and disappeared. When Commander Tereth gave her the news, it had been all she could do not to break into song. Those few days had been glorious. Aside from keeping some Bajoran woman they'd captured sedated, her tasks had been minimal. She had been able to get through *Burning Hearts* twice.

Unfortunately, the captain found the *bolmaq* on Narendra III, and it had been back to the nightmare.

Perhaps, she thought, *I'll be lucky and she'll die on San-Tarah.*

That happy scenario now lodged in her head, Gaj skipped ahead to her favorite part of the novel.

*The smell of Lughor's blood on her hands suffused
Ngara's senses; she longed to flick her tongue in his
wound, greedily lapping the droplets from his skin.
Hunger for her burned in his dark eyes. Pinning her arms
above her head, Lughor slid his d'k tahg blade beneath
the lacings of her leather corset, blade against breast. "I
will have you!" he growled. And with a swift up-thrust—*

"I will be released from this place—*now!*"

Gaj looked up in annoyance. Lieutenant Rodek
was sitting up in his biobed. The nurse tried and
failed to remember what the lieutenant had been
brought in for. She supposed that she could look it
up, but that required more effort than she was willing
to go to.

Not that it mattered. She didn't have the authority to release patients, nor did she particularly wish
it. If she wanted responsibility, she would have become a doctor instead of a nurse.

"I can't release you, Lieutenant. You'll have to
wait until Dr. B'Oraq—"

"That was not a request, *Nurse*. That was an
order. You will fetch me my uniform."

Gaj sighed, and put down her padd. Lughor and
Ngara would have to wait. "Sir, I cannot release you
without—"

"I am giving you an *order*, Nurse!" Rodek's voice
was raised so loud, Gaj swore the bulkheads shook. "I
am captain of this vessel, and you will obey me without *question!*"

Without even realizing that she'd gotten up, Gaj

found herself standing at the closet where patients' uniforms were kept while they were interred in the *bolmaq*'s dungeon. She removed Rodek's uniform and handed it to him.

Rodek took the armor from her so fast the edges scratched her hand. Gaj, however, did not cry out in pain, finding herself afraid of what Rodek would do to her if she did.

However, the gunner did nothing except glower at her with a pitiless stare, blink once, and then exit the medical bay without comment.

The nurse let out a breath she hadn't even realized she'd been holding. *Some patients are determined to leave no matter what.*

As she applied a salve to her hand, she wondered at Rodek's referring to himself as captain of the vessel. *He's just a lieutenant—the first-shift gunner. Why would he say to me that he's the captain?*

It was possible, of course, that it meant he was addled and not fit for duty, but Gaj found herself not caring all that much. That sort of thing was the *bolmaq*'s problem, not hers. She just wanted to get back to *Burning Hearts*—she was just getting to the good part....

"Get us out of here!"

Klag cursed even as he gave the order. He hated having to run, even if only for a moment, but an exploding warp core was not something he wished to be near. Ideally, the *Gorkon*'s shields would be sufficient defense against the matter-antimatter explosion, but the shields had been weakened in battle, and the structural-integrity field was still under repair.

Kornan said, "Course 287 mark 9, Leskit— execute!"

"I'm executing, I'm executing," Leskit muttered, barely loud enough for Klag to hear. Klag also saw that the *Kreltek* was taking a similar course: away from San-Tarah, and also away from the *Akua*'s makeshift weapon.

A moment later, the warp core exploded in a fiery plume that was quickly consumed by the vacuum of space.

"Sensors down," Toq said. "Clearing now."

"Bring us back, Commander," Klag said to Kornan.

"Yes, sir. Reverse course back to San-Tarah."

Klag frowned as he stared at the viewer, which had a visual display that told him nothing, thanks to the effects of the subspace eddies. "Toq, position report on all ships."

Toq read off from his console display. "*Kreltek* on parallel course with us, returning to the planet. *K'mpec* still drifting at fifty thousand *qell'qams* from the planet. *Jor, Nukmay,* and *Khich* have engaged the *Taj* and the *Gogam* in orbit." He looked up. "No sign of the *Vidd* or the *Akua.* Some of the subspace eddies have shifted position as well, sir."

"Keep trying to locate the *Vidd* and the *Akua,* and map the changes in the eddies. Meantime, we will proceed to aid Captain Huss." Three birds-of-prey, even with as talented a warrior as Huss in command and the benefit of disruptors, were no match for a battle cruiser and a strike ship.

Kornan came over from the gunner's position and stood to Klag's right. In a tone low enough so that only the captain could hear, the first officer said, "Sir, the *K'mpec* is adrift. We should finish them off as we did the *Tagak*."

"No."

"Sir—"

His voice a virtual hiss, Klag said, "Are you questioning my orders, Commander?"

"Of course not, sir, but—"

"I will *not* give the order to kill my own brother." Klag took a breath. "If we are to meet face-to-face in battle, or if the *K'mpec* fires on us again, I will not hesitate to act, but I will not strike my own blood down unprovoked. Nor will I order others to do it for me."

"As you say, sir."

"Rodek?"

That last was Toq's voice. Klag turned around to see that Rodek had in fact entered the bridge. He was in full uniform, with one of B'Oraq's healing devices still on his head.

Klag rose from his chair, standing alongside Kornan as they both stared at the new arrival. "Lieutenant? B'Oraq told us that you would not be able to return to the bridge for several days."

"I am fit for duty, sir. I would ask that I be allowed to take my station."

The captain took all of a millisecond to mull. B'Oraq was on San-Tarah and in no position to counteract the order, and Morketh and Grint were both dead. He needed an experienced gunner at the controls. "Take your post, Lieutenant," Klag said, turning back to the viewscreen.

"It is good to have you back," Klag heard Toq say to the gunner. "We have put off our celebration for far too long." Then, more loudly, Toq said, "Sir, I have located the *Akua*. It is in orbit—their shields are down!"

"How soon until we are in range?"

"Six minutes," Leskit said.

"Transporter activity, sir," Toq then said. He looked up. "General Talak is beaming more ground troops to San-Tarah!"

"Alert *QaS DevwI'* Vok as soon as we are in range," Kornan said.

"Increase speed, Leskit," Klag said, returning to his chair.

"Sir, the eddies—" Kornan started.

Klag smiled. "I trust Leskit to avoid them. The *Akua* is vulnerable—we must strike *now* and cut off the beast's head so that the body may wither and die."

"Now at full impulse," Leskit said.

A minute later, Rodek said, "*Akua* now in weapons range."

Kornan turned to his captain. "Your orders, sir?"

"Expedite that *petaQ*'s journey to *Gre'thor*, Commander."

"Full disruptors on the *Akua*, Lieutenant," Kornan said, "and fire."

As Klag watched, the *Gorkon's* disruptors shot forth onto what was left of the *Akua*. With its port wing destroyed, its running lights at half thanks to their lack of a warp core, the ship reminded Klag of a bird he'd seen once on a hunt he and Dorrek had gone on with their father. M'Raq had downed a *targ*. As they were moving to collect it, a low-flying *ramjep* bird swooped down and got in the way. Klag's father swiped at the avian with his *d'k tahg*, cutting open its wing. Now, the *Akua* looked like that wounded *ramjep* trying desperately to stay aloft as it lurched through the air away from the hunters and the *targ*.

Moments later, the *Akua* exploded in a fiery conflagration.

Clenching the very same fist that had wounded the *ramjep* years ago, Klag smiled with satisfaction.

"Sir," Toq said, "we're receiving a report from Vok. The *Akua* beamed down a thousand troops—led by General Talak."

Klag's smile fell.

As long as Talak lives, honor will not win the day.

CHAPTER TEN

"**C**h'drak to Wol."

Wol activated her communicator. She stood in the small hut at the center of Val-Goral talking with Je-Ris, the head of this village's ruling pack, about how to defend the city. They had just received word that more troops had beamed down from the *Akua*. This changed the balance considerably. The reinforcements sent from the *Taj*, which had a much smaller complement of troops than either the *K'mpec* or the *Gorkon*, served mainly to make up for the considerable casualties among the *K'mpec*'s original deployment. But the *Akua* was a ship of roughly the same size as both the Chancellor-class vessels, with a like complement of troops. Even with the added benefit of having the Children of San-Tarah on Captain Klag's side, these new troops would make the campaign in general and holding Val-Goral in particular much more difficult.

"What do you want, Ch'drak?"

"*Since you are remaining here, there is someone you should speak to immediately. A prisoner.*"

Frowning, Wol said, "He is conscious?"

"*Yes.*"

A Klingon warrior who consciously allowed himself to be taken prisoner was an honorless coward. This meant that he was bound for *Gre'thor* when he did die. Of greater moment, however, was the fact that honorless cowards also made excellent interrogation subjects. "I will join you shortly."

She concluded her business with Je-Ris, ordering her to deploy both Klingon and San-Tarah troops along the upper ridge to prevent anyone else from attacking the city the way Wol herself had. Then she proceeded toward the command post. As she stepped out of the hut, she inhaled the smells of battle: the blood of both Klingon and San-Tarah mixing freely with the scents of the dirt and the native flora and fauna—marred only by the chemical stink of G'joth's grenades, and that was dissipating. She regretted that Krevor had not lived to see this glorious combat. It might have even been sufficient to satisfy the ever-contentious Davok. And even if it hadn't, Wol found that she missed his complaints.

"*B'Oraq to Wol.*"

"What is it, Doctor?"

"*Goran has arrived with your prisoner, but I'm afraid he didn't make it. Your mek'leth did its job too well.*"

Wol cursed.

The doctor continued. *"Vok has asked me to tell you that he's keeping Goran in the Prime Village—the fighting has gotten fierce, and he is needed here."*

"Of course," Wol said. She had expected as much as soon as word of the general's beaming down with more troops had come to her.

"I take it you wish me to dispose of the body."

At that, Wol hesitated. Normally, there would be no question, but there were other issues. *How to explain this to her? Will I even be able to?*

Should I?

Then B'Oraq added, *"After taking a blood and tissue sample, naturally."*

Cautiously, Wol asked, "Why would you wish to do that, Doctor?"

"Because I am neither blind nor stupid, Leader. You and the prisoner share a crest, which means you may share a bloodline. Since I know for a fact that your service record indicates that you have no known family, and since I am relatively sure that no prisoner would truly be worth having Goran haul him all the way here, I assume you wish me to perform a genetic test."

Wol shook her head. *Damn the woman for her efficiency.* On the other hand, she doubted that any other Klingon doctor would understand her request, much less accede to it. "If you wish to take a sample before disposing of the *bekk*'s body, Doctor, that is certainly within your purview. If there is anything it can tell you about the soldier that you think might interest me, I would be grateful if you would share it."

"Of course, Leader. And I promise discretion, as well. There is a Federation concept relating to the practice of medicine about confidentiality between doctor and patient. I have found it to be generally impractical in the Empire, but under these circumstances, I believe that particular aspect of my Starfleet Medical training will prove—beneficial to us both."

"Thank you, Doctor. Out."

Wol ended the communication, but her apprehension increased. Lokor had already indicated to Wol that he knew she was truly Eral, daughter of B'Etakk, last survivor of the now-disgraced House of Varnak. *Or, at least, one of the last survivors. Now B'Oraq would probably know as well. Of course, she has access to my medical records, and could determine my bloodlines in an instant if she wished. Still, she would have no reason to make such an investigation of one of the thousands on board—until now.*

B'Oraq was a revolutionary, attempting to bring improved medical practices to the Empire. Her job was made easier since Martok's ascension to the chancellorship, as his regime favored such inclinations, but that did not change the fact that she was trying to bring about a radical change. Such people were dangerous ones to trust, because their cause tended to be the sole consideration in how they dealt with others. Wol had to be careful to ensure that her own secrets would not be conscripted for B'Oraq's crusade—either as a weapon or a means to use Wol in some other way. The Leader also had to consider that B'Oraq had the support of Captain Klag, and any move against the doctor would put Wol in the most precarious of positions.

Damn you, Father, for reducing me to this.

She approached the command post and forced all thoughts of the House of Varnak to the back of her mind. Ch'drak stood before her, a tall, imposing figure with a comparatively weak crest and an unimpressive beard. *Here's another one I must be careful of.* Ch'drak was the highest-ranking Leader among *QaS DevwI'* Klaris's squads, the second group of squads, with Wol as the last among Vok's, the first group. There were some who would consider Ch'drak's position to be more prestigious than Wol's, but Wol could not count on Ch'drak not being among them. Her own short-sightedness had provided an opening for Ch'drak, and now she needed to be careful that he did not take the opportunity to sink his *d'k tahg* into it.

Next to Ch'drak stood two soldiers who were holding a third. A white-haired old warrior, he wore the emblem of the *K'mpec* on his chestplate and the rank of *bekk* on his biceps.

Ch'drak said, "This old razorbeast has chosen not to die in order to provide us with intelligence of a traitor in our midst."

"You lie!" the old man said, spitting blood onto the ground. "I will be more than happy to die—*after* I have shared my information with your pitiful selves. And I am *not* telling you of a traitor."

Laughing, Ch'drak said, "That is what it sounded

like you said before the Leader arrived. Do you now change your story to suit your needs? Are you a Ferengi?"

The old man's laugh was just as derisive. "Your pitiful attempts to insult me are typical of such honorless *petaQ* that ally themselves with animals over true Klingons." He cast an eye over to a group of San-Tarah who were speaking several meters away.

Wol stepped forward. The old man smelled of blood and day-old *raktajino*. "We ally ourselves with honor, *Bekk*."

"You go right on thinking that, woman."

She gave him a backhanded slap across the jaw, causing more blood to fly from his mouth. "I am Leader Wol of the fifteenth, *Bekk*. You will address me with respect."

"None from your ship of fools deserves respect," the prisoner said before spitting out a bloody tooth.

"Then why do you claim to provide us with intelligence?"

"Because I want you to know the depths of your stupidity before I go to *Sto-Vo-Kor*. What I told this *yIntagh* here," he nodded his head toward Ch'drak, who, to his credit, did not react to the insult, "was that I had information about one who had provided intelligence to *us*. In fact, if you are Leader of the fifteenth, it is one within your very squad."

Wol of course knew that there was a traitor, but for it to be one of her own distressed her. *It can't possibly be Goran, and I doubt it's G'joth. That left Maris or Trant.*

Her initial instinct was Trant—he was a malcontent, after all, and he had questioned this entire endeavor. But that was simply talk—it proved only that Trant was annoying, not a traitor.

Then she remembered Maris's insistence that they not change their plan, his inability to see the patterns of the *QoSbow* wielders despite how blindingly obvious they were. That was *not* simply talk, those were actions, possibly ones designed to keep Wol from changing a battle plan. *Why would he do that unless he had reason to want the plan to remain unaltered?*

"Maris," she said, as much to see how the prisoner reacted.

The prisoner's eyes bulged, thus confirming Wol's suspicion. "You—you knew? But—but how? I.I. agents are never—"

At that, Wol whirled on the prisoner and grabbed him by the chestplate and pulled his face even closer. At this range, she revised her estimation of his breath to contain week-old *raktajino*. "*What* did you say?"

"Your *Bekk* Maris is a patriot—an agent of Imperial Intelligence sent to root out dishonorable behavior. I would say that going against the chancellor's chief of staff in battle qualifies."

Maris is I.I.? That cannot be . . .

The prisoner wasn't finished. "He was giving us information using a tight-beam transmitter that used an I.I. code. Our *QaS DevwI'* have been receiving his reports since we arrived on this mudball. But he is no traitor, and neither am I—it is all of *you* who will be consigned to the Barge of the Dead for choosing to follow a dishonorable *toDSaH* into—"

Wol cut off his diatribe by stabbing him in the chest with her *d'k tahg*. "Dispose of this filth," she said after removing her blade. Then she activated her communicator. "Wol to G'joth. Find Trant and Maris, have them report to the command post."

"I'm with Trant right now, Leader," G'joth said. *"We'll be able to come, but Maris won't—he's dead."*

"Dead?" Wol felt as if the dirt was collapsing under her feet. First Maris was a traitor, then an I.I. agent, now a corpse. *All this right after I finally found my son and killed him. It's been quite a day.*

"Yes, Leader. It looks like one of—one of my grenades went off unexpectedly. He's been ripped to pieces by shrapnel."

"Do not touch the body," Wol said. "What is your position?"

"We are behind the hut belonging to the smith."

"I will join you immediately." She turned to Ch'drak. "Je-Ris is deploying troops. Coordinate with her—we may be under attack at any moment from General Talak's forces."

"Of course, Leader," Ch'drak said with an oily smile.

I will definitely have to watch out for that one, Wol said. Like a hunter scenting a wounded *targ*, Ch'drak was now ready to move in for the finishing blow. She would need to remind him that a wild animal was at its most dangerous when wounded.

Finding the smith's hut was easy enough—just

pick out the stench of smelted metal from the other odors that competed for olfactory attention and follow it. Within minutes, she found G'joth and Trant standing over a body. She looked down to see Maris covered in blood, with metal shards having ripped open parts of his arms, legs, and head. Most notably, one jagged piece of metal protruded from the remains of his right eye.

"Search the body," Wol said. "He may have a transmitter on him."

"What?"

"Before being sent to *Gre'thor* where he belongs, one of the *K'mpec* troops informed us that they have been receiving tight-beam transmissions from an I.I. agent in our midst."

G'joth laughed. "Maris? With I.I.? That's absurd."

Shaking his head, Trant said, "I have served with Maris for many turns, Leader. He is *no* agent of Imperial Intelligence. They have higher standards than that."

"Don't be a fool, Trant," Wol snapped. "Do you truly think I.I. would send an agent who was incapable of convincingly disguising his true self?"

Trant shrugged. "I suppose not."

G'joth, meanwhile, had commenced searching the body. "There's a *d'k tahg,* a ration pack, a few other components that probably could be assembled into a weapon on another planet—but no transmitters that I can see."

Wol frowned. "Keep his body under guard. I want

it brought back to the *Gorkon* when this is over." She turned to Trant. "How did he die?"

Trant looked down. "Foolish happenstance. We were approaching the hut when one of these grenades went off unexpectedly. He bore the brunt of it." He turned to G'joth. "If you had constructed weapons that *worked* properly, fool, then Maris would still be alive!"

"To betray us again?" G'joth said. "Besides, these are chemical explosives. The reactants don't always mix at the same rate—or sometimes the bottle doesn't break open, but only crack. Had you been actually paying attention when you were instructed on the grenades' use instead of whining like a Ferengi about—"

"Enough!" Wol said. "Both of you, be silent!" She thought quickly. If the death was accidental, there was less of a chance of reprisals from I.I. But if he was there to sabotage the *Gorkon*'s mission, such reprisals were still a risk.

This is more than I should have to deal with. In truth, there was no reason for her to do so. For now, there was battle. If they lived through this day, she would deal with the consequences then.

Or, rather, her superiors would. "We will hold the body for Lieutenant Lokor. This is now a security matter, so *he* can deal with it. Then we will prepare for battle. General Talak's troops will be here soon. Trant, pick up the body."

* * *

The Imperial Intelligence agent who went by the name Trant bent over to pick up Maris's body. Of course, G'joth had not found anything because Trant had already removed the stolen I.I. transmitter from Maris's person.

Trant breathed a sigh of relief as he did so, however. Maris's "accidental" death meant that the *Gorkon* crew would think that one of the I.I. agents on board—and everyone knew that a ship the size of the *Gorkon* had at least a few agents in place—was no longer a problem. In particular, one who would betray them to a *petaQ* like Talak.

In truth, Trant supported Klag's actions. The general's command to force Klag to go back on his word went against everything the Empire stood for. True, the expansion into Kavrot was important, but the Empire's strength in the next few years would come from the return to the glory days of honor that Martok was spearheading in the wake of the Dominion War and the failed coup. In order for that movement to succeed, the Empire could not afford to cast aside the teachings of Kahless so cavalierly, not even in the name of necessary expansion.

So he had taken the opportunity to test his fellow warriors, playing the malcontent to give them a target, someone to justify their position to, and thus reinforce it to others who might be vacillating.

But he had not counted on Maris. Somehow—probably during the night Maris had spent in the bunks assigned to the fifteenth while Trant rotted in the medical bay—the *toDSaH* had gotten his hands on the I.I. transmitter Trant kept among his belongings. Since Trant had not needed it, he had not checked to see if it was present.

He only knew Maris had stolen it when Maris came to him shortly after the howls of the Children of the San-Tarah and the victory cries of the Klingons indicated that they had taken Val-Goral.

"We have to leave," Maris had said then.

Trant blinked in confusion. "What?"

Maris repeated, "We have to leave. Come, my friend, we can go together. They'll take us in on the *K'mpec*."

"What are you talking about?" Trant asked, though he was starting to suspect.

"I have been providing the *K'mpec*'s forces with information. But with this setback, we cannot remain with that *petaQ* Wol anymore."

"How have you been providing this—information?"

Laughing, Maris said, "With your transmitter, of course. You *are* I.I., yes? I found your transmitter, and I thought I would aid you in your task. General Talak will be very pleased, don't you think?"

Trant had never thought much of Maris. Indeed, he thought less of the *bekk* the more he got to know him, thinking him an ordinary soldier who was astonishingly easy to manipulate. Certainly he played along nicely when Trant had picked a fight with Maris in front of Wol a week earlier. It set in motion the chain of events that put Trant under Wol's command. That had been Trant's goal from the moment the former daughter of B'Etakk reported on board.

Obviously, Trant needed to upgrade his opinion of Maris—or lower that of himself for letting this imbecile get his hands on an I.I. transmitter. Trant immediately injected a dose of *vIHbe'* into Maris's neck, which paralyzed him. The *vIHbe'* would only last a few minutes before it broke down and became both inert and undetectable, even in an autopsy, but it was more than long enough for Trant to toss a grenade into the air and run away. When the grenade landed a meter to Maris's left, he could not duck the blast, and was cut to pieces by the shrapnel. By the time G'joth came to see what caused the explosion, Trant had removed the transmitter from Maris's dead body.

Now, however, Maris was dead, as was his accuser, according to Wol. If any others made the accusation, there was no evidence to back it up one way or the other, so Trant was not in any danger from his superiors.

He could carry out his assignment as planned.

"Tactical report."

At Klag's order, Kornan turned to the gunner station. "Lieutenant?"

Rodek nodded and put an overlay on the viewer. Klag saw San-Tarah represented as a large red ball. Around it was a latticework of lines representing the subspace eddies. The original configuration of the eddies was in dark blue, with the eddies that were newly shifted after the *Akua* warp-core explosion shown in a much lighter blue. In green were the ships now on Klag's side, with what remained of Talak's fleet in yellow.

Rodek reported: "The *Kreltek* and the *Vidd* have joined the *Jor*, *Nukmay*, and *Khich* in battle against the *Taj* and the *Gogam*."

Klag saw that the birds-of-prey remained mostly unscathed, but also had inflicted little damage. The *Kreltek* had only just joined the fray, and was in good condition, but the other three could not say the same. They were on the verge of annihilating each other.

And Talak is on the planet, rallying his troops, no doubt.

"Sir," Toq said, "we are receiving a report from *QaS DevwI'* Vok—and Me-Larr."

"On speaker."

Vok's voice was barely audible, as the speakers suddenly became awash in the sounds of battle—the metal-on-metal clanging of blades and warriors screaming. "*Captain, we are holding the outer villages, but the Prime Village is being overrun. General Talak has sent most of his troops here.*"

"*I do not understand this strategy, Captain Klag,*" Me-Larr added. "*We are many—why focus the attack on one village?*"

"Symbolism, Me-Larr," Klag said. "Plus, it is best to take the center of governmental power first. The rest of a world will fall into line after that."

Me-Larr seemed genuinely baffled. "*Vok said the*"

same thing. That is absurd. The Prime Village is simply a place. We live off the land. If the land is no longer useful, we find another piece of land."

"*Sir,*" Vok said urgently, "*what are your orders?*"

Klag looked at the tactical display. The addition of the *Kreltek* was turning the battle in his favor. Neither the *Taj* nor the *Gogam* would be in any condition to fight for much longer. Captain Huss had taken her ships to the periphery. Her specialty was surgical strikes, after all, so this engagement—

Suddenly, Klag threw his head back and laughed.

"*Sir?*" Vok asked.

"Captain," Kornan said, "what is—"

Waving his first officer off, Klag said, "Vok, listen to me carefully: You are to retreat from the Prime Village. All Klingons and San-Tarah are to retreat. How long will that take?"

"*Ten minutes—perhaps longer, given that some will wish to remain behind and continue the battle.*"

"If they do, they will die well." Klag turned to Toq. "Contact Captain Huss and tell her to prepare for atmospheric entry and attack." Then he turned to Kornan and grinned. "The Prime Village is about to become—no longer useful."

After a second, Vok laughed a hearty laugh, and Kornan also smiled.

"I have Captain Huss, sir," Toq said.

"*I am sounding the retreat now, Captain,*" Vok said. "*And sir—I request that we be granted twenty minutes, so we can activate the transporter blockers we took from*

Val-Goral. It will prevent the general from a cowardly withdrawal of his own."

Klag bared his teeth and rumbled his approval at this use of the general's own weapon against him. "Twenty minutes, Vok. *Qapla'*."

"Qapla', *Captain*."

Me-Larr added, *"I thank you once again, Captain Klag. Your stories will be told in every season that is yet to come."*

The captain took some satisfaction in the fact that, on one world at least, his deeds would be enshrined. He was half-convinced that the only song that would be composed in the Empire about this day would have a title along the lines of the "The Day Talak Faced the Traitors."

Huss's face once again appeared on his viewscreen, her red hair—and the bridge behind her—in a bit more disarray than it had been when last they spoke.

"Captain," Klag said, "you said you were willing to fire on General Talak once again. I am now giving you that opportunity. You are to set course for the Prime Village on San-Tarah and raze it to the ground. Time your arrival so that the attack does not begin for at least twenty minutes."

"Talak has always had a tendency to allocate his resources poorly. Committing the bulk of his troops to the Prime Village is a weakness—you are wise to pursue this strategy, Captain."

"I am glad you no longer find it lacking."

186

For the first time, Klag saw the woman smile. *"Not at the moment, anyhow. We are changing course and reconfiguring for atmospheric entry. I will contact you again when the Prime Village is destroyed. Out."*

Even as the viewer returned to the tactical display, Klag turned to Kornan. "In the meantime, we will join the battle here."

Kornan nodded. "Leskit, set course 111 mark 2. Time to arrival?"

"With the new configuration of the eddies—thirty minutes."

"Attempt to reduce that time frame, Leskit," Klag said.

"I'll do what I can, Captain, but no promises."

An interminable amount of time passed as they worked their way around the newly arranged subspace eddies. At one point, Rodek said, "We'll be in weapons range in ten minutes."

"Prepare a disruptor barrage," Kornan said.

Rodek then looked up. "Sir, the *K'mpec* is drifting into one of the subspace eddies. They are showing minimal power. If they drift much farther in, they will be destroyed."

That brought Klag up short.

Dorrek.

Kornan asked, "How long do they have, Lieutenant?"

Rodek studied his console for a moment. "Four minutes."

The first officer then fixed Klag with a look, but

Klag found that he could not read it. But then, he had yet to be able to truly read Kornan. And there was nothing the commander could say at a time like this in any case.

On this matter, Klag stood alone with his thoughts and memories....

"Why are you here, Dorrek?"

"Let us praise the one who allowed her captain to soil the memory of a great warrior by stitching his remains onto the shoulder of an unworthy fool."

"Surely, you have not come to wish your older brother well on his induction into the Order."

"There is blood between us, and it will not end until one of us is in Gre'thor."

"What do you know of a Klingon way of life, Klag? You, who mount our father's arm to your shoulder like some kind of sick trophy?"

"Whether you like it or not, I am head of our House, and that gives me every right to instruct you. Now, in the name of the House of M'Raq, I order you to join us. Face the general down. Remember that a Klingon's word is his bond, and without it, we are nothing."

"My duty, brother, is to obey the orders of my superiors. That is something you will never be."

Over a decade ago, Klag told William Riker that a Klingon was his work, not his family. "That is the way of things," he told the human. Klag used those words to justify the reasons he would not see M'Raq after his father returned from the Romulan prison camp and awaited death on Qo'noS.

Now he had to put those words to the test. The captain of the *K'mpec* was his enemy, now. Dorrek had chosen—against Klag's direct order as older brother—to side against Klag in a matter of honor. Klag had had no compunction about seeing the *Akua* destroyed, of course, nor the *Vornar*, the *Kalpak*, the *Gro'kan*, or the *Tagak*. They, too, were the enemy, as were the *Gogam* and the *Taj*.

Klag knew in his heart, his mind, his very being that his course was the right one. It was the path of honor, the one that both his father and his brother had rejected. Dorrek had disgraced their House, and deserved nothing but death.

"We are not on our own, brother—we are together. We are the sons of M'Raq. Is there nothing we cannot do?"

He stared at his right hand, as if it contained the spirit of his and Dorrek's once-proud father, as if it would provide some insight to Klag now. *Should I leave Dorrek to his fate—drifting lazily to his doom? Or should I move to rescue him, at least give him the opportunity to die fighting?*

"Sir," Rodek said suddenly, "the *K'mpec* is firing thrusters."

Turning to look at the viewer, Klag saw the *K'mpec* no longer drifting. Its running lights had dimmed even further, but the aft thrusters now kept it at a steady distance from the eddies.

Toq then said, "Sir, *QaS DevwI'* Vok is communicating from the service."

"This is Klag, Vok—report."

The troop commander's words were barely audible over the all-encompassing sound of metal blades slamming into each other, or into armor, or into flesh. The noise of battle seemed to fill the bridge. "*Sir, the Prime Village has been razed—but General Talak still lives, as do many of his troops. There are reports of heavy fighting in the outlying villages.*"

Again, the captain looked at his father's arm. Klag had never believed in destiny or fate or in higher beings that provided guidance. The only guidance he needed was from Kahless. But now, events had conspired to remind him of his true mission.

He was an inductee of the Order of the *Bat'leth*. It was his sworn duty to uphold the words of Kahless and keep his fellow warriors on the path of honor.

His foe was not Dorrek, though Dorrek had allied himself with his enemy. No, Dorrek was not the true heart of this battle.

Talak was.

It was Talak who put Klag in the position of going back on his word. Talak who made a mockery of Klingon honor. And Talak whom Klag needed to concern himself with now, not Dorrek. *For a Klingon is his work—not his family.*

"Continue to hold the line, Vok. I am beaming down to take charge."

Everyone on the bridge turned to look at Klag in surprise.

Turning to his first officer, Klag continued: "Commander Kornan, you are in charge of the *Gorkon* until my return. Do everything you can to insure our victory in space."

Kornan started to say one thing, stopped, and then said, "Yes, sir."

Without another word, Klag turned and left the bridge, his bodyguard falling into step behind him.

It is time to end this.

CHAPTER ELEVEN

B'Oraq finished putting together the splint on the Child of San-Tarah's arm, administered a hypospray, admonished him to be careful, secure in the knowledge that the advice would be ignored, then sent him on his way to return to battle.

It is much like treating Klingons.

She had been forced to abandon the *HoSpI'tal* when Vok gave the order to retreat from the Prime Village—though she would likely have lost it anyhow, since if they had not retreated, Talak's forces would probably have overrun the place. She knew Talak's doctor aboard the *Akua*—a butcher who, B'Oraq knew, used his medical knowledge to instruct warriors on how best to kill their opponents rather than to heal—and assumed that the general would not be amenable to such a facility as hers.

Then again, most Klingons aren't. That's why there isn't even a word for it in the language.

They had set up camp in the same clearing in front of a cave opening where over a week ago Klag had met with the Ruling Pack and decided that San-Tarah's fate would be determined via the martial contests. *Or so everyone believed at the time,* B'Oraq thought bitterly. Now the cave was her *HoSpI'tal.*

She could hear the sounds of explosions far away: Vok's troops using those grenades that *Bekk* G'joth had put together. B'Oraq lamented the loss of so many specimen bottles, but she was hardly in a position to refuse their use, given the tactical advantage it provided. Luckily, she had not depleted her entire supply—one still sat safely in her belt with material she intended to test on behalf of Leader Wol. *I wonder what she expects me to find.* If Wol were male, she would assume the dead soldier to potentially be a long-lost son, but B'Oraq didn't see how a Houseless woman could have a son and not remember it. *Unless she simply did not report the birth when she enlisted.* It struck B'Oraq as odd, but who truly understood how lowborn Klingons thought?

"You are the healer!"

This statement of the obvious came from a white-furred Child of San-Tarah. She was holding a black-furred male, bleeding profusely from wounds in his neck and chest.

"Put him down over here," B'Oraq said, pointing to the ground next to one of the medikits she had assembled for use on this nightmare of a planet where only half of her electronic equipment functioned.

As she set him down—somewhat roughly—the woman said, "His name is Bo-Denn. You will save him."

B'Oraq started to examine the wounds, which were parallel. The chest wound was smaller than the neck wound, and based on the angle and the depth of both it looked to have been made by a single *bat'leth*, wielded by a left-handed Klingon swiping downward. "I'll do my best, but—"

"You must save him!" the woman cried. "He took a blow that was intended for me. I would be dead if not for him, and you must save him so I can ask him why!"

At that, B'Oraq looked up. "Why would he not?"

The woman hesitated. "I am El-Yar. When your people arrived, Bo-Denn and I were settling a dispute. He stole a keepsake of mine, then denied it. I was well on the way to defeating him in combat when you arrived to invade us."

The chest cut was not serious—B'Oraq quickly put a field bandage on it, which was sufficient for the nonce—but the neck wound hit an artery. She would need to repair it if El-Yar's request was to be fulfilled.

Despite herself, though, she was curious as to El-Yar's words. "What does this have to do with what just happened?"

"Bo-Denn is a thief." El-Yar spoke as if B'Oraq was a fool for not understanding. "And he lies to the Ruling Pack and to me. How can one such as he then be responsible for giving his life for mine? It makes no sense."

It does if he never stole the keepsake, B'Oraq thought, but did not say so aloud. She was far too busy trying to repair Bo-Denn's artery without the benefit of autosuturing tools. The Starfleet Medical Academy had, of course, included training in emergency medicine that covered this sort of eventuality, but that didn't make it any more pleasant for her to mechanically apply the bonds that would hold the artery together to facilitate the body's natural healing ability. She opened a bottle of alcohol and poured it over the wound to sterilize it.

"So you must save him," El-Yar said, "so I may ask him why he did this."

"He did this because you are fighting a war," B'Oraq said. She winced as she spread the skin and fur of Bo-Denn's neck apart to expose the artery. As she did so, blood spurted out—the artery had a long cut of at least fifteen centimeters in length. She had to get the bleeding under control. "That supersedes any petty personal concerns."

El-Yar stared directly at B'Oraq. "I suppose it would, but—" She turned to face the cave wall. "He has never behaved like this."

"Your people have never faced a situation like this." Even as she spoke, she started sealing the cut as best she could, her hands now covered in Bo-Denn's blood up to her wrists. "Your very world is at stake. This is not the time for holding grudges."

"It's just another fight," El-Yar said dismissively.

"When it's over, we must resume our combat and resolve our dispute."

You poor fool, B'Oraq thought as she leaned back and cleaned out the blood from the wound. *With any luck, that was the only bleeder.*

"El-Yar," she said without looking at the woman, "your entire world has changed irrevocably. Don't you see it?"

"That's stupid. Nothing has changed. We fight, then we go on with life as before."

B'Oraq wondered how many of the Children of San-Tarah believed that, and was worried that the number was higher than those who did not. She finished cleaning the wound, saw that the bleeding had stopped, and then bandaged the wound carefully, applying a salve that would facilitate the skin's healing.

"Centuries ago, Klingons thought we were alone in the universe. Then the Hur'q came. A vicious species, they ravaged our planet from space, stole our treasures, and were never heard from again. From that day on, we knew that the universe had changed. The world was no longer Qo'noS, it was the entire galaxy. If we were to remain strong—if we were to remain *Klingons*—we had to face that galaxy head-on. Now we are one of the great powers of the quadrant."

As B'Oraq turned her attention to more properly treating the lesser chest wound, she continued. "Our arrival will have the same effect on your people, El-Yar. *Everything* has changed, and you can never go back to life as it was before."

The doctor looked up to see El-Yar staring at her. B'Oraq didn't know enough about San-Tarah body language to be sure, but she was relatively certain that El-Yar's expression was one of incredulity. "That is absurd. Life is always as it was before. That is the way of things."

"He must rest," B'Oraq said, standing up and going to a water basin to clean her hands. "And if you believe that the way of things will remain constant, you may do so. But I suspect you will be surprised—if you live through this—to find that it never will be."

"He will recover?"

"Yes."

El-Yar turned to leave. "Good."

"Oh, and El-Yar?"

She turned back around.

"If you think things won't change, why did you bring Bo-Denn to me? Healing abilities such as mine are *not* the way of things, after all."

To B'Oraq's lack of surprise, El-Yar had no response to that. Instead, she simply turned back around and left the cave.

Sighing, B'Oraq finished washing the blood from her hands and face, then went outside. The sounds of battle grew louder, though removed from the wounded in the cave, the smell of blood became less intense.

The red glow of a transporter beam heralded the arrival of Captain Klag and his bodyguard. He was, she noticed, armed with a *mek'leth*, a one-handed weapon that he could wield without the deleterious effects of a right arm that was still not fully integrated with the rest of the captain's body—no matter how much the captain might wish it otherwise. Had Klag armed himself with a *mek'leth* instead of the *bat'leth* he did use when he fought Me-Larr in the deciding contest with the Children of San-Tarah, he might well have won, the *Gorkon* crew would have been victorious, and San-Tarah would already be part of the Klingon Empire. *And El-Yar and Bo-Denn might have been able to settle their dispute.*

"Preparing for battle, Captain?" she asked.

"Yes," Klag said with a smile.

"Only this time with the proper tool for the job, I see."

"I should think, Doctor, that by now you would know that I do learn from my mistakes."

Now B'Oraq returned the smile. "Eventually, Captain, yes, you do."

Me-Larr, Ga-Tror, and Vok approached. "What are your orders, sir?" the latter asked.

"Continue as you have. I am going to speak to Talak."

Ga-Tror made an odd noise. "After all this, Captain Klag, in the end you call out a challenge to your enemy?"

"Yes."

"For all your posturing, for all your 'technology,' you are still much like us in the end."

Klag again said, "Yes. It is why I thought you worthy to be given my word—and why I have fought so hard to make sure that it was kept."

"And that is appreciated, Captain Klag," Me-Larr said. "You have done as great a service to the Children of San-Tarah as any fighter, any member of the Ruling Pack, even as any god."

Laughing that infectious, throaty laugh of his, Klag said, "Say that when we are victorious, Me-Larr."

The captain then stepped forward and activated his communicator. The former motion was unnecessary, but it put Klag at the forefront of the clearing in front of the cave, which was surrounded by rocks and boulders and had only one uphill approach. It made no difference to the person Klag planned to contact, but B'Oraq assumed he did it for the morale of his own soldiers.

"Klag to Talak."

It was a moment before the general replied. "*I have nothing to say to you, Captain. You have won nothing this day.*"

"Perhaps not yet. But you are outnumbered here: we have superior weaponry, we know the terrain better, and we have air support. You are outnumbered in orbit as well."

"*For now, perhaps. But I have the entire fleet behind me. You and your fellow traitors will not have the advantage long.*"

"I disagree—both with your conclusion and that we are traitors. And that is the heart of this conflict between you and me, is it not? I offer you a proposal."

B'Oraq heard the contempt in the laugh that

Talak gave in response. *"Are you a Federation diplomat now, Klag?"*

"No, I am simply giving a general in the Klingon Defense Force a chance to salvage an honorable victory from what would otherwise be an embarrassing defeat. After all, I assembled my fleet less than three days ago, and yours has been together since the heyday of the war—and now you stand on the brink of defeat, in part because you could not even keep all your own ships fighting on your side. Some might say that this is proof that honor will always win the day—but I will leave such musings to the clerics and the opera composers. For now, I offer you a choice." Klag turned to Me-Larr and smiled. "On this world, they settle disputes by combat within a circle approximately six meters in diameter."

"And you wish to offer this instead of continuing combat?"

"Yes. You can stay on this course, and almost surely lose—or face me alone in battle." Klag now started to pace. "Enough warriors have died today because of our disagreements—Klingon and San-Tarah blood has flowed freely, and it has been a day worthy of song. But now it is time we ended it. What say you, General? What legacy will you leave behind?"

For many long seconds, there was no reply. Only then did B'Oraq realize that the sounds of combat were now muted—a clang of blades here, a scream there—but nearby, at least, much of the fighting had ceased. B'Oraq suspected that Klag had made sure that his challenge to Talak was heard by all the Klingons on the planet. Now they awaited the words of their respective commanding officers as to whether or not the battle was to continue.

Finally, the general spoke. *"The only thing I intend to leave behind, Captain, is your corpse. We will meet in this circle of your* jeghpu'wI' *friends."*

B'Oraq cheered. Vok joined in, and Me-Larr led the Children of San-Tarah in a long howl.

K'Vada could feel the heat of several console fires warming his face. The bridge seemed to be coming apart around him—a microcosm, based on the reports Yivogh had been giving him from engineering, of how the *Vidd* was coming apart around the bridge.

"*Gogam* coming in for another attack," Yivogh said. "Shields are now at ten percent!"

Cursing, K'Vada said, "Evasive! Have we regained targeting ability?"

"No, sir, we—"

Yivogh's words were interrupted by another console exploding.

Even as automated fire control combined with officers wielding extinguishers to try to contain the blazes, the bridge was rapidly becoming uninhabitable, and functionally useless. None of K'Vada's status boards were working, and the pilot was pounding furiously and futilely at the helm control.

"Shields are down," Yivogh said from the operations console—the second officer and gunner were both dead. "Weapons are still offline—and matter-antimatter containment is failing!"

Again, K'Vada cursed—this time a very long curse in the ancient tongue of their ancestors, one that K'Vada's great-grandmother B'Akko had taught him when he was a child. "It is a powerful curse," the old woman had cautioned him then. "It summons one of the old gods from the dead in order to bring about misery. Only use this curse in the most dire of situations, boy, you hear me?"

I hear you, B'Akko. It doesn't get much more dire than this. . . .

The viewer was functioning only sporadically, but when it did work, it showed the *Gogam*. About two-thirds the size of the *Vidd*, it had only an eighth of the crew. The remaining space was given over to a massive collection of weapons arrays, cannons, and torpedo launchers. Such strike ships were an invaluable part of any fleet, and K'Vada had been grateful that two of them were taken out by Klag's secret minefield early on, as it increased their chances of victory a hundredfold.

Unfortunately, with the *Kreltek* and the *Taj*—both *K'Vort*-class ships—trading blows and being more or less evenly matched, and Huss's ships called to the surface of San-Tarah, that left the *Vidd* to the *Gogam*, and K'Vada wasn't making nearly as good a show of it as he'd have hoped.

"Sir," Yivogh cried, "engineering reports we cannot contain the breach! We'll need to eject the core!"

K'Vada looked around his near-useless bridge. If they ejected the core, they'd be in the same position as the *K'mpec*—adrift, in danger of falling into orbit, drifting into one of the eddies, or simply being finished off by the *Gogam* or the *Taj*.

No.

He turned to the pilot. "Set collision course with the *Gogam*, maximum impulse." He turned to Yivogh. "Tell engineering to arm all torpedoes manually and to set the disruptor cannons to overload."

"Containment breach in thirty seconds," Yivogh said. "Time to intercept *Gogam*—" The first officer looked up and laughed. "—thirty seconds."

Our god has risen from the dead and is about to cause the Gogam *some misery.* K'Vada turned to the viewer and grinned. "Today is a good day to die."

The warp core breached, the disruptors overloaded, the *Vidd* collided with the *Gogam*, the torpedoes exploded, and they all perished. K'Vada's last thought as the explosions took him away was amusement that—after all these years in which no foe could stop him—he had to take it upon himself to die well.

Talak stood in the circle, gripping his *tik'leth* with both hands.

He was starting to understand what it was that the captain saw in these creatures. The so-called Children of San-Tarah were indeed magnificent fighters, and came from sensible, if primitive, traditions like the ones he and Klag were making use of now. They engaged in combat with a fire, a passion, and a skill that put even many of his own soldiers to shame.

And this world! A lush paradise, with pure skies, verdant fields that were ripe for the hunt! This was a place to bring your children, to teach them the way of the warrior, to bring them pure combat in a way that was increasingly harder to do on other Empire worlds, especially in the wake of the war's devastation.

To Talak's mind, these features made it all the more imperative that San-Tarah be brought into the Empire by any means necessary. *Imagine what these creatures, armed with disruptors and protected by proper armor, could have done against the Jem'Hadar. The Dominion War would have ended* months sooner. Talak remembered when the Dominion retook Chin'toka: They had been outnumbered and outgunned. Captain Yovak's troops were overrun on Chin'toka IX after successfully holding the planet for months. If she had had warriors such as these under her command, with their ferocity, their spirit...

No, for Klag to have allowed them to escape becoming part of the Empire so easily proved that the son of M'Raq was the greatest fool of all.

Around them, maintaining a respectful distance, was a crowd primarily made up of Klingons, with some Children of San-Tarah mixed in amid those from Klag's crew. Talak noticed that many of the two score members of Captain Huss's crew had joined the throng of *Gorkon* ground troops as well. *When this is over, Captain, you will pay a thousandfold for your be-*

trayal. Huss was a member of the House of Rozaj, a strong family that controlled several manufacturing concerns relating to communications technology—and one whose prosperity was due as much to Huss's accomplishments as anything. *Not for much longer,* Talak swore, thinking about how those manufacturing concerns would benefit the House of K'Tal....

But such thoughts were for after, for when the battle was recalled over bloodwine and *racht.* Now Talak needed to study his foe. The general had not been in Klag's presence since the day on Ty'Gokor when Martok had provided the captains of the Chancellor-class vessels with their assignment to the Kavrot Sector, and then he had paid little heed to the captain. After all, Klag had built his captaincy on the grave of a worthier warrior, that of Talak's Housemate Captain Kargan of the *Pagh.*

Klag was taller and younger than Talak, and had a reputation as a fierce fighter. However, he was armed only with a *mek'leth,* which had a shorter primary blade than Talak's weapon. Talak also suspected that the captain's right arm—grafted onto Klag's form as onto some kind of automaton—would not provide the range of motion of the one the captain was born with.

"So," Talak said, holding his *tik'leth* in a defensive posture, holding the hilt over his heart with the blade straight upward pointing toward the sky. "You believe that you can defeat me as you did those Jem'Hadar you claim to have slain on Marcan V?"

Talak never believed the tales of Klag supposedly killing a dozen Dominion soldiers and their Vorta handler during the war. Armed only with a *mek'leth* after his arm had been cut off in the *Pagh*'s crash, the tale went, Klag slew them literally single-handedly. The general had seen many battles in his time and also seen the operas based on those selfsame battles; rarely did the events of the two intersect. Talak was quite sure that either Klag downed the Jem'Hadar with both arms, and only lost the limb afterward—or perhaps during the battle—or, more likely, that he had nothing to do with the deaths of the Jem'Hadar. Klag had been rescued by Captain Ganok of the *Rokronos*, and the general knew him to be an inveterate exaggerator.

Klag, however, did not rise to the bait. "I do not *claim* anything, General. What deeds I have committed in the past are of no consquence to what we do today. All that matters is that you have dishonored me. Now one of us will pay the price for that dishonor."

"The price has already been paid," Talak snapped angrily. "The blood of thousands of warriors has been spilled today because of your imagined dishonor. And what do you know of honor anyhow? You who sew foreign arms to your body and take credit for the deeds of greater warriors. The House of M'Raq's gains after Marcan rightfully belonged to the House of K'Tal. *That* is truly the dishonor that will be righted this day, Klag—for you and your House will no longer profit on Kargan's carcass."

Klag threw his head back and laughed. "You, who

claim to be of the same family as that fat old *toDSaH*, can truly stand there and call him a greater warrior while maintaining an even composure? But then, you are one who disregards a Klingon's word of honor as if it were of no consequence."

Talak smiled. "You misunderstand, Captain. I consider the word of a Klingon to be of great import. It is *you* who are of no consequence."

The captain scowled, which only made Talak's smile grow wider.

"Enough." Klag moved to a defensive posture, holding the *mek'leth* blade horizontally over his chest. "It is time to die."

Talak swung his sword, but Klag parried it easily, the metal striking metal with a clanging sound that echoed off the surrounding trees. They each backed away a step. Klag then swung his *mek'leth*, and Talak parried just as easily. Right now, they were taking each other's measure.

They each made progressively bolder strokes. Talak realized that, whatever Klag's faults, he knew how to wield a *mek'leth*. He used the longer blade aggressively, yet managed to use the smaller blade defensively, protecting his sword arm while keeping the general's straighter, long single blade from getting through. *Perhaps he did not truly slay a dozen Jem'Hadar, but he would probably be able to hold his own against them.*

The early stages of a swordfight were always the most cautious; one attempted to learn how one's opponent fought, seeing what strokes and parries were used. Klag's attacks and defenses were fairly standard, but executed with impressive skill.

Soon, however, Talak found the pattern he was looking for: Klag used the *mek'leth* one-handed. Specifically with his right hand. *I need to get him to further expose his left side.*

The general allowed Klag to back him toward the edge of the circle. *A line drawn in the dirt—how prosaic.* And yet, truly, no more was needed. Still, Talak saw room for improvement. *When San-Tarah becomes part of the Empire, we may adapt this for our own use. Only the circle will be maintained by a lethal forcefield.*

Once he reached the edge, he pressed the attack, focusing almost entirely on Klag's right. Klag parried each thrust, though his response time, Talak noted, lessened with each stroke. On the seventh such thrust, Klag came close to losing his footing as he thrust the *mek'leth* out and to his right to stop it.

Talak took advantage of that to take a swing to Klag's left, which was now completely exposed, especially with the captain's momentary loss of footing. The sword sliced into Klag's armor.

The blood roared in Talak's ears as the battle lust overtook him—first blood was his!

Then he growled in agony as a sharp pain sliced into his left shoulder, right at the joint of his own uniform. It was a weak spot that only the most skilled—or the luckiest—of swordfighters could penetrate, but Klag did so, after Talak had committed to the left strike.

"*Qu'vatlh*," Talak muttered as he yanked the sword out of Klag's side with his right hand, his left arm now hanging uselessly at his side. A fire burned in his left shoulder, yet he had no feeling in the arm below the biceps. He could not make his hand flex or his arm move.

Klag had sacrificed first blood in order to strike a crippling blow.

The *tik'leth* could still be wielded one-handed, but the strength of his strokes was greatly reduced, as was his dexterity. Angrily, Talak slashed at Klag, a blow the captain easily ducked, but Talak pressed the attack.

"How?" the general asked as he slashed at Klag's neck, which Klag blocked. "How have you done this?" Another slash, this time at the chest, also blocked. "You convince Martok that you are the great warrior instead of Kargan." Another. "You perform arcane surgeries on your person and are not ostracized." Another; this time Klag simply dodged it. "You turn one of my most loyal captains against me, and overwhelm my superior forces in space."

Klag blocked another stroke, but this time he did so by catching the *tik'leth* blade between the two blades of his own *mek'leth*. Snarling, Talak tried to disengage his own weapon, but Klag then redirected the blow downward, then quickly back up, slamming the hilt of his *mek'leth* into Talak's face.

Talak stumbled backward, spots dancing in front of his eyes, the glorious taste of blood filling his mouth from a tooth that had been dislodged.

Then Klag smiled, and quoted the words of Kahless. " 'When honor is at your back, it matters not who your foe is. You will be victorious.' "

During the war, Talak had journeyed many times to the Federation space station designated Deep Space 9. Martok, then holding what was now Talak's position as chief of staff, had offices there, and he directed the Klingon war effort from the station. On one such visit, Talak had heard the station's commander, a human captain named Sisko, say that sometimes the devil would quote scripture to his own ends. The quote had made no sense—Klingons had no true equivalent for this human devil—but Sisko explained the metaphor.

Hearing Kahless's words from the filthy mouth of the son of M'Raq called that human aphorism to the general's mind now. Talak swore he would never let those lips sully the great words of Kahless again.

Screaming loud enough so that his dead crew could hear him in *Sto-Vo-Kor*, Talak ran forward to attack Klag once again.

Kornan stood at the forefront of the *Gorkon*'s bridge, grinding his teeth in annoyance at having to watch the *Vidd* and the *Gogam*'s final confrontation while still being too far away to do anything about it. The battle was in a location that, thanks to the subspace eddies, was still too far away for the *Gorkon* to reach for another five minutes.

He silently wished Captain K'Vada well on his

journey to *Sto-Vo-Kor.* Kornan swore he would not have died in vain.

All that was left was the *Taj,* which was currently trading blows with the *Kreltek.* Despite having been in the fight longer, the *Taj* was making a better show of it. The *Kreltek* had lost its forward shields and had shut down half the ship to conserve power. Kornan suspected that Captain Vekma's relative inexperience—she had been captain for less than a day, after all—was proving her undoing.

What does that say about my joining her, when I have less than nothing in terms of such experience?

"How soon, Leskit?" Kornan asked impatiently.

"I'm moving as fast as I can—firing range in one minute."

"Rodek, train all available forward disruptors on the *Taj.*"

Even as Rodek acknowledged the order, Kornan saw that the *Taj* was firing its disruptors on the *Kreltek.*

Leskit frowned. "That isn't good."

"Toq?" Kornan prompted. The *Taj* should not have been able to fire its disruptors, since the *Gorkon* did not share Kurak's breakthrough until after that vessel's treachery.

The young second officer shrugged. "Kurak is not the only talented engineer in the fleet, Commander. If she could determine a way to fire disruptors, so too could the *Taj*'s engineers."

"*QI'yaH,*" Kornan muttered.

Toq added, "The *Kreltek* has lost shields—they

have hull breaches on multiple decks." He looked up. "They're dead in space."

"In range," Rodek said.

"Fire!" Kornan cried. "Leskit, put us between the *Taj* and the *Kreltek*. Do not allow them to apply the finishing blow."

The *Taj* fired right back, even as they took damage, then turned.

"The *Taj*'s course is taking them out of orbit—into the eddies."

"Pursue," Kornan said at Toq's report. "Tactical on screen."

The viewer changed to a display that gave the eddies in blue. Kornan saw that the *Taj* was heading into a section where several eddies had converged in response to the *Akua*'s warp-core explosion. It was a tangle of eddies that the *K'Vort*-class ship would barely be able to navigate, and which the larger *Gorkon* would be even harder-pressed to handle.

Kornan looked over at Leskit—his comrade from the *Rotarran*, his rival for Kurak's fickle affections here on the *Gorkon*—and knew that if anyone could get them through it, it was him.

"Maintain pursuit, Leskit. We will not let the traitor win the day."

"That would be bad, Commander," Leskit said. "I need to reduce to one-quarter impulse."

"Do so."

The *Taj* flew through, missing one of Rodek's mines, which disappointed Kornan. He had a flicker of hope that they would hit the mine—Klag had never revealed their precise location even to his allies—but they did not. *That just means that we will have to finish them ourselves.*

"Sir," Rodek said seconds later, just as the *Gorkon* flew close to the same mine, "*Taj* is firing disruptors—at the mine, sir!"

Kornan felt the blood roar in his ears. *Damn them!* "Reverse course!"

But it was too late. The disruptors set off the mine, and the explosion tore through the *Gorkon*'s port shields.

"Damage report!" Kornan screamed over the dozens of alarms that suddenly went off.

"Port shields down!" Toq said.

"Helm control gone," Leskit said. "We're drifting into—"

Kornan had no idea what the rest of Leskit's sentence was to be, as a plasma junction exploded, sending Kornan forcibly to the deck. His ears rang as his head collided with metal, and he tasted his own blood in his mouth as he got up.

Getting to his feet, he saw that the explosion had sent Leskit careening to the front of the bridge. The old pilot was not moving.

Immediately, Kornan ran to helm control. He stabbed at the panels, but they would not respond. The displays still worked, however, telling him that they were inside one of the subspace eddies. Kornan was able to instruct the computer to backtrack their course, and he saw that the mine explosion had only minutely affected their course, but Leskit had been so carefully navigating the eddies that even the slightest course change would send them careening into the deadly tears in space.

Then, all of a sudden, helm control functioned again. Kornan immediately instructed the engines to reverse course and take them out.

Out of the corner of his eye, he also saw that another plasma junction was about to go. But the helm controls were far too sluggish to be put on autopilot, and the piloting necessary far too precise; once they were on course, he needed to keep them there until they caught up to the *Taj* and were free of this tangle of eddies. The eddies altered the very fabric of space around them, causing gravitic shifts that necessitated constant corrections just to maintain course. It could not be trusted to a computer, especially one not functioning at full capacity.

The *Gorkon* was now back on the course Leskit had plotted, but Kornan still could not afford to take his eyes off the console.

Behind him, he could hear voices, but he could not focus on them. Toq and Rodek were saying something about damage and shields and things, but Kornan ignored it. The slightest distraction would send the *Gorkon* back into an eddy.

Focus.

He heard the sound of an explosion.

Focus.

Pain sliced through his chest and torso. Fire seared his belly. He ignored that, too.

We're almost through.

In another ten seconds they would be clear of the worst of the eddies, and also in firing range of the *Taj*.

Focus.

His vision blurred, but he refused to even blink to take his eyes off the display.

Almost there.

Then, at last, they were clear.

"Sir, I said I can take over now!"

Kornan turned to see that Ensign Koxx was standing next to him. Moving out of the ensign's way, Kornan said, "Set course for the *Taj*, full impulse." He wanted to move back to the center of the bridge, but suddenly his legs wouldn't work. Undaunted, he continued giving orders. "Rodek, full spread of disruptors. I want that vessel annihilated. Toq—"

Then Kornan's legs gave out completely. All feeling left his body, so he did not actually feel himself hit the deck, though he could now only see the ceiling of the bridge, so he knew he must have fallen down.

It was only as Toq stood over him saying something—*Why can I not understand him?*—that Kornan realized that the explosion had killed him. But he hung on until the ship was out of danger.

I have died saving the ship. It was a far worthier death than he had imagined for himself, and for the first time he allowed himself to have hope that he would go to *Sto-Vo-Kor* after all.

His only regret was that he never did get the opportunity to take Kurak to his bed....

For the first time, Klag's right arm felt comfortable.

It wasn't something he had ever noticed before. He assumed the discomfort he'd felt since having his father's arm grafted on was due to his having grown accustomed to only one limb for so long. But the weeks passed, and the discomfort remained.

Now, though, fighting Talak with his *mek'leth* gripped in the right hand of his father, it felt *right*. As he blocked the general's *tik'leth* strike, it truly felt like he was defending himself with his own arm.

Or perhaps it was because of what Talak said to him. Until Talak had asked his plaintive query, Klag had not thought of himself as a victor here.

For all he spoke of honor and of not allowing Talak to betray his word given to a worthy foe, the fact of the matter was they had gotten into this mess, not because of honor, but because of pride.

No, not pride—what is the human word that Riker shared with me? Hubris. The Klingon word *Hem* indicated a sense of accomplishment and self-worth. But the human term had a connotation that would never occur to a Klingon: pride that blinds, pride that is out of proportion to the reality of the universe.

Klag's hubris brought them to this place. Dorrek had conquered a world, accomplished the mission

Martok had set out for them. He had found a planet that was worthy of being brought under the Empire's boot, and had called in Talak's fleet to complete the job of conquering it. When Klag found a world that was even better, he could not allow himself to be satisfied with just that. So when Me-Larr proposed the contests that would provide him with the chance to conquer the world without the help of the general's fleet—or, more to the point, without the help of the general himself—he leapt at it.

And then, the final blow, his own foolishness in using a two-handed weapon in the final conflict against Me-Larr in a circle much like this one when his *bat'leth* skills were not up to the task.

B'Oraq had warned him. *She's a sorceress, that one; she sees, where I am blind.* She knew that his true motives lay in jealousy of his brother for succeeding, in hatred of Talak and what his Housemate Kargan did to Klag for all those agonizing years on the *Pagh*, and, ultimately, in his disdain for the way his father chose to meet his death. But Klag did not heed her words— indeed, he broke her arm for her effrontery—and it led to this. Klingon fighting Klingon and San-Tarah, the dirt of this world awash in the blood of Klingon and alien alike, and a conflict that divided warriors in their very hearts.

Yet here was Talak, marveling not at his pride, not at his foolishness, but at his triumph. *My path is that of honor, whatever my motives may have been.*

The sounds of metal clanging against metal filled

the air, slicing through the noises of the crowd around them. The warrior cries were indistinct, though Klag could occasionally hear specific importunings of himself and Talak both, as their loyal troops cheered on their commanders.

Talak's attacks became slower, sloppier. With only the use of his right arm, he had lost precision. He was of sufficient skill, and his blade of sufficient strength and reach, that this loss of precision still made him a dangerous opponent—and Klag had his own problems, as the pain of his wound slowly spread from his left stomach to his entire torso.

Right now, he held his wound shut as best he could with his left arm and elbow. It made for slightly awkward positioning, but he did not need his left arm to fight with the *mek'leth,* and he preferred to slow the process of bleeding to death as much as possible.

Slowly but surely, Klag went on the offensive, parrying then thrusting, then thrusting again, then not needing to parry at all. Talak's defenses were strong, but Klag would not let him go back on the offensive.

Seeing this, the Children of San-Tarah began to join the cheers of the *Gorkon* crew with howls to the sky. Klag swung his *mek'leth* down toward Talak's head, but the general parried it, linking his blade into the area between the *mek'leth*'s two blades.

"Listen to them," Talak said with a sneer. He stood now on the edge of the circle, his right arm holding their weapons in place. "They are *animals!* You would die for such as them?"

"I would die to safeguard my honor, Talak. I gave Me-Larr my word. The word of a Klingon warrior is enough to move planets, to destroy starships, to annihilate suns! But without it, we are *nothing!*"

"What of the word you gave when you swore an oath to serve the Klingon Defense Force?"

Klag smiled. "I swore to uphold the traditions of our people, Talak, as did you. And one of our oldest traditions is that when a superior officer is derelict in his duty, he is to be challenged and removed."

"Challenged, perhaps." Talak laughed. "Removed? Never! Not by such as *you!* I am Talak, son of Yorchogh of the House of K'Tal! I have served the Empire all my life! You are the filthy son of a cowardly *petaQ*, a usurper of honor, and an affront to all that Klingons stand for! I will not be defeated by you!"

The captain locked eyes with his foe even as the general screamed his curses. Though the words were laden with the venom of a *wam* serpent, that venom did not spread to Talak's steely gray eyes.

Klag saw fear.

As far as Klag was concerned, the battle ended right there.

Talak did not take joy in the glory of combat. His heart did not sing the song of battle. Instead, he knew only that he might lose, and could not face that reality, instead hiding behind churlish invective.

The general had the use of only one arm because his left had been injured beyond his capacity to use.

Klag had the use of only one arm because he chose to use his left arm to keep his wound closed.

Reaching up with his left hand, he gripped the hilt of his *mek'leth*. Even as pain racked his torso as the wound opened further, Klag, with the added strength the second hand gave him, twisted his wrists to the right. That broke Talak's one-handed grip on his sword, and it fell to the ground.

Undaunted, Talak threw a punch toward Klag, but the captain intercepted the blow with his left hand, then slammed the hilt of his *mek'leth* into Talak's face with his right. Talak fell backward, out of the circle. Blood ran into his brown beard from his nose and mouth.

With a cry that echoed off the trees, Klag shoved his *mek'leth* into Talak's chest.

The light left the general's gray eyes a moment later.

Now there were only two sounds coming from the crowd: Klingons rhythmically chanting the name of Klag and Children of San-Tarah howling the victory to the heavens. After a moment, Klag heard one soldier begin to sing the Warrior's Anthem, another chant the first verse of "Don't Speak," a third beginning the aria from some opera or other.

Klag knelt down and pried open the eyes of his enemy.

In that moment, he felt everything. The jealousy of Dorrek, the disappointment in M'Raq, the hatred for Kargan, the anger toward Talak, the frustration with Kurak and Kornan, the joy of battle, the sorrow of betrayal—all of it seethed and boiled and flowed in his stomachs, building into a growl.

He lifted his head up to the heavens, to the clear blue sky of San-Tarah, to the subspace eddies that blotted the stars from view, to the sun that the world orbited, to the entire Kavrot Sector and the Beta Quadrant beyond it.

And he screamed.

The scream overwhelmed the chants, the howls, the singing.

General Talak was on his way to *Sto-Vo-Kor.*

And Captain Klag was victorious.

Klag screamed until he no longer had the breath to scream.

Then he screamed some more.

Exhausted, he finally stopped, put his left arm back over his wound, and clambered to an upright position.

"Klag! Klag! Klag! Klag! Klag! Klag! Klag! Klag! Klag! Klag! Klag! Klag!"

The cheers were leavened only by the howls of the Children of San-Tarah. And Klag found that he saw no Klingons who were *not* chanting, not even those of General Talak's fleet.

Truly, the battle had been won.

More or less, he thought, remembering that there were still several ships in orbit. Klag yanked his *mek'leth* from the chest of the shell that once contained Talak, sheathed the weapon, and activated his communicator. "Klag to *Gorkon.* Report."

"This is Toq, sir. I was about to contact you. Commander Kornan is dead—and a vessel has just decloaked outside the eddies."

Klag wanted to laugh. *Has another member of the Order answered my summons?*

But Toq wasn't finished. "It is the Sword of Kahless, Captain. We are being hailed by Chancellor Martok."

EPILOGUE

Ambassador Worf stood in the large meeting room of the *Sword of Kahless*, at once disappointed and satisfied.

The former was because he had missed the battle—and a glorious battle it had apparently been. Seventeen ships engaged in battle, with only seven left intact—and two of those seven, the *Kreltek* and the *K'mpec*, would need extensive repairs at a drydock before they were again spaceworthy.

The latter, though, was because his own contribution was the right one. Martok had known nothing of the goings-on in the Kavrot Sector until Worf brought them to his attention. Without a moment's hesitation, and with several choice comments regarding General Talak, the chancellor ordered his flagship to be readied. He had not been able to leave immediately, as several affairs of state needed to be dealt with or formally postponed, but he had departed Qo'noS as soon as he was able.

He also requested that Worf join him.

At first, Worf was going to refuse. His position as Federation ambassador gave him no real standing here. This conflict was internal to the Empire and involved territory neither claimed by nor indeed anywhere near Federation interests. He quite literally had no place on this mission.

Then Martok had said, "I am not asking the Federation ambassador to accompany me, my friend. I am asking a member of the Order of the *Bat'leth* to escort his chancellor to the site where the Order is doing its work."

Leaving Wu in charge at the embassy, Worf joined Martok on the *Sword of Kahless* without another thought.

He had, naturally, spent the entire journey to the Kavrot Sector catching up with his paperwork.

Now he stood in the meeting room, just to Martok's right. A small version of the Council Chambers in the Great Hall, the dark, high-ceilinged room (it took up two decks' worth of space, an indulgence few Defense Force vessels would have, but this *was* the flagship) was backlit to emphasize the Klingon trefoil on the wall behind the large chair where Martok now sat. The medal-covered cassock of office draped over the chair's arms as the one-eyed chancellor listened to Klag—standing in the room's center—give a full verbal report of what had happened.

Also present, standing opposite Martok and against the far wall, were the two other surviving ship captains: Huss and Vekma. The *Taj* had no one in command at present. The ship had come at the behest of Commander T'vis, the first officer, but it was also he who betrayed Klag's fleet to General Talak. T'vis then killed B'Edra and took over the *Taj*, then gave the order to cease hostilities with the *Gogam* and fire on the *Qovin* and the *Ch'marq*. When the *Sword of Kahless* decloaked and Klag announced that he had killed General Talak, the *Taj* second officer immediately challenged and killed T'vis, but also died from wounds incurred in the duel.

Worf remembered B'Edra from the induction ceremony on Ty'Gokor and, while he was glad to know that she had not betrayed Klag, he was saddened that her death came at the hands of so unworthy a creature as T'vis.

Finally, standing in a corner was Me-Larr, the head of the Ruling Pack of San-Tarah, who managed to look overwhelmed and defiant at the same time. He had a warrior's bearing, though, and Worf started to understand what it was that Klag saw in these people that led him to the decisions he made. His furred form and protruding snout reminded Worf of the wolves that prowled the forests in the valleys of the Ural Mountains on Earth.

The only part of Klag's account that gave Worf pause was personal—when Klag mentioned that

Rodek had come up with a method of mining the subspace eddies in orbit around San-Tarah. According to Klag, Rodek claimed that it was something that had been done on the *Hegh'ta*—except Worf knew that Rodek, son of Noggra, never served on that vessel.

Kurn, son of Mogh, however, was captain of that ship once, years ago. It was at a time before Worf was cast out of the Empire by Chancellor Gowron for opposing the latter's invasion of Cardassia in the dark days before the Dominion War. Before Kurn was also cast out, a victim of Worf's dishonor. Before Worf had authorized a procedure that would alter Kurn's memories and physical appearance, making him over into Rodek. The procedure that Dr. Bashir had performed on Deep Space 9 should have erased all of Kurn's memories.

Yet now he was recalling missions from the *Hegh'ta*.

Worf knew that this would need to be addressed sooner or later. For now, however, he chose later, hoping that fate would not decide to go against that choice.

Finally, Klag ended his report with the part that all present already knew: The *Sword of Kahless* decloaked, the *Taj* and the *Gorkon* stood down, and all Klingons were beamed up from the surface of San-Tarah, with the sole exception of B'Oraq, whom Me-Larr and another of the Ruling Pack, a woman named Te-Run, had requested be left behind to tend to the wounded, along with a few *Gorkon* troops.

"Your choice was the right one, Captain," Martok said after Klag finished. "Your actions were just and honorable."

"Thank you, Chancellor," Klag said with respect.

"Me-Larr, step forward."

The head of the Ruling Pack did so. "You lead the Klingons' Ruling Pack?" Me-Larr asked formally.

"Yes. I am Martok, son of Urthog. On behalf of the Klingon Empire, I offer our regrets at what has happened here. The actions of General Talak were wholly—"

Me-Larr interrupted. "You do not need to explain, Chancellor Martok. Captain Klag has taught us many things about your people—both directly and indirectly. You have nothing to regret. You have acted true to yourselves, and those who have acted untrue have been dealt with appropriately."

Martok smiled, and Worf couldn't help but crack one of his own at that expression. Almost any other chancellor would have chafed at the interruption, at the effrontery. But Martok had no such airs, and he appreciated that Me-Larr was forged from similar metal. "In that case, Me-Larr, we will simply take our leave of you, as promised by Captain Klag. The Klingon Empire will never set foot on San-Tarah again."

"That is not required, Chancellor Martok."

Every face in the room turned toward Me-Larr in surprise then. Worf frowned. He had spent many years dealing with many different alien species, and one could not always determine what a new species' body language indicated. However, Worf was fairly sure that Me-Larr had come to a decision, and was now implementing it. Worf saw none of the sense of being overwhelmed now, only the defiance. *Not only has he made the decision, he will challenge anyone who brooks it.*

"I have consulted with Te-Run. She is the keeper of our traditions and laws. Captain Klag will vouch for the fact that she is wise, perhaps the wisest of the Children of San-Tarah."

Me-Larr looked to the captain for confirmation, and Klag nodded guardedly. *He is as baffled as the rest of us,* Worf thought.

"We have learned a great deal since Captain Klag and his vessel appeared in our sky. We have been exposed to the universe outside our world. We have seen wonders and tools beyond our wildest imaginings. We have been in fights that make the conflicts of old seem like minor skirmishes. We have seen both the best and the worst of your people. We have had our entire way of life turned inside out, and we have triumphed. But that triumph has changed our world forever, and we would be fools to cast it aside now."

Worf noticed that, as Me-Larr paced around the center of the room, he never once made eye contact with any member of his audience. "Our contest with Captain Klag was based on who triumphed in at least three of the five contests. Captain Klag's people defeated us in the hunt and in capturing the prize. The Children of San-Tarah were victorious in wind boat combat and in strength. That left only the final battle between myself and Captain Klag in the circle. Tradition demands that the two combatants fight until death—or until one of the combatants leaves the perimeter of the circle. As Captain Klag informed you in his report, I disarmed him and he was at my mercy. I spared his life, for truly I did not wish to kill so fine a fighter."

Me-Larr then stopped pacing. "Te-Run, however, has informed me of my error. As I said, the tradition of that particular fight states that the loser is the one who is killed, or who steps outside the confines of the circle. After I spared Captain Klag's life, I stepped outside the circle."

Now Me-Larr looked Martok directly in the eye. His posture was seemingly relaxed, but Worf saw that the San-Tarah's arms were positioned in such a way that he could easily reach the hilt of his curved, double-bladed sword on its back holster.

"Therefore, as established in the terms of the agreement the Ruling Pack made with Captain Klag, I lost the fight, and the Children of San-Tarah lost the competition. I hereby cede the world of San-Tarah to the Klingon Empire."

Me-Larr's words echoed off the high ceiling and faded. Then silence descended upon the meeting hall. The head of the Ruling Pack stared at Martok, who returned the favor by fixing his one eye on Me-Larr.

After several tense seconds, the silence was broken by a hearty, throaty laugh. Worf turned to see Klag, his head back, his laughter cascading up toward the ceiling.

A moment later, Martok joined in the laughter, as did Huss and Vekma. For his part, Worf simply smiled.

"I accept your words, Me-Larr," Martok said. "A planetary governor will be assigned to begin the integration of your world into our Empire." Martok looked to Klag. "And, based on what the captain has told us, perhaps also integrate our Empire into your world. I suspect that there is much we can learn from each other."

"Chancellor, may I speak?"

Worf looked up to see Captain Huss stepping forward.

Martok nodded affirmation. Me-Larr stepped aside to stand near Klag, and Huss moved to the middle of the room.

"I wish the assignment of planetary governor. I had expected to receive the honor at Brenlek, but General Talak chose Captain Worvag instead."

Again, Worf smiled. Huss's tone indicated precisely how little she thought of this Worvag and his assignment as Brenlek's governor. The ambassador wondered if that contributed to Huss's eventual betrayal of General Talak, if he denied her the post she wanted. Also her current position as part of Talak's fleet had obviously come to an end, since her three birds-of-prey—as well as the three left behind at Brenlek—were all that remained of that fleet.

"Besides," Huss added, "it would be fitting to be the one who supervised the construction of a new Prime Village, since it was I who destroyed the old one."

Martok nodded. "Fitting indeed, Captain. Very well, you are so assigned. The *Jor*, *Nukmay*, and *Khich* will remain behind as support and you may request other vessels to assist you as needs be."

"Thank you, Chancellor."

"Captain Vekma," Martok said to the dark-haired woman. "The *Kreltek* will be towed back to the repair base on Cambra III. I want you to take command of the *Taj*. There is a vacuum in leadership on that vessel, and Captain Klag has spoken highly of you."

Vekma shot a look at Klag and smiled, showing a mouth full of long, pointed teeth. "Has he?"

Klag nodded at the captain—who, Worf recalled, served with Vekma on the *Pagh*—and smiled.

"I wish to bring Commander Hevna with me, sir. She is the Order member who alerted me to Klag's plight, and allowed me to remove an honorless *petaQ* from his unworthy position on the *Kreltek*."

"Very well," Martok said. "I believe that concludes the business we need to attend to. Captain Klag!"

Klag stepped forward.

"You have done well. There are those who would question your actions, but you can be assured that I am not among them. It is exactly for this purpose that the Order of the *Bat'leth* was created." Martok leaned back in his chair, the medals on his cassock rattling. "I will be assembling a new fleet. In the meantime, you will continue your mission into the Kavrot Sector."

"Sir, we will need crew replacements. We lost many officers and troops."

"Of course. You may take personnel from the *Kreltek*. And Captain?"

"Yes, Chancellor?"

Martok grinned. "Perhaps next time, you can find us a world that can be conquered *without* turning the Empire on its ear."

Klag returned the grin. "I will do my best, sir."

"See that you do."

After Martok dismissed them, Worf moved toward the exit. He had more paperwork, after all. However, Klag approached him, intercepting the ambassador before he could leave. "It would seem I owe you a debt of gratitude, Ambassador."

"Not at all," Worf said. "In fact, I did not follow the letter of your message, since your imploration was for fellow Order members to join you. I was not in a position to do so."

"Instead, you did the next best thing. Would that Martok had arrived sooner, but I suppose that the business of the Empire is not something that can be easily dropped."

Worf nodded. "Indeed. I am glad that I was able to contribute."

Klag slapped Worf on the shoulder. "That you were, my friend. Oh, and you will be happy to learn of who I have chosen to replace Kornan as my new first officer...."

Klag sat in his office on the *Gorkon*, watching as the *Sword of Kahless* maneuvered carefully through the subspace eddies in order to take the *K'mpec* in tow. Elsewhere, Vekma was doing the same with her new command in order to tow her former one. All four ships would then proceed to the Cambra system.

Seeing the *K'mpec* drifting helplessly, its barely working thrusters the only thing keeping them from a fatal encounter with one of the eddies, Klag knew there was one duty he had to perform before the *Gorkon* and the *K'mpec* went their separate ways.

He opened a communication to his brother.

"Ah, yes," Dorrek said. *"I was expecting this. Have you called upon me to gloat, Klag? To lord your superiority over me?"*

"In fact, I have not." Even as he said the words, Klag wondered why he *had* called. What did he have to say to his brother now, after all, that had not already been said? Still, he felt he had to talk to him once more before they parted.

"I do not see why. You should declare victory—you have won most decisively. You have defeated me, prevented me from an honorable death, instead forcing me to limp home in disgrace, towed by the flagship like a vole in the teeth of a grishnar cat. You have killed a great man with the right arm of our father, and made noble warriors betray their oaths of duty. Our House falls further and

further into dishonor, but Klag—oh yes, Klag has done well! Klag has won! Klag has once again used others to prop up his own accomplishments! Kargan, Worf, Picard, and now Martok, all have paved the way for Klag to gain prominence!" Dorrek leaned forward. "*Congratulations on your grand victory, Captain. You should have sealed it by killing me, because I will not rest until you have paid for what you have done to me, to Talak, and to our family this day."*

"Our family? The only one who has disgraced us is you, Dorrek." Klag rose to his feet. "I pitied you, once, because you strayed from the course of honor, but now I see that that was wasted. You have not just strayed from the path, but rejected it! Talak, Kargan—these are not great men, they are misbegotten animals from a House whose time has passed. Talak's last words were an insult to our father—the very one whose honor you have falsely claimed to be defending by rejecting me. By allying yourself with such as him, you prove yourself an even greater disgrace, and worthy of nothing but my contempt."

"*Then that, at least, we share, Klag, for you have nothing but my contempt."*

Sitting back down, Klag said, "That is *all* we share, Dorrek. I am the head of our House, and as such I have decided that you will no longer be part of it." Klag hadn't even realized that he'd come to the decision until he said the words.

He paused, considered, then realized that it was his only recourse. He had hesitated in battle because

Dorrek was his brother, and it could have cost them. In fact, so much of what happened at San-Tarah was because of how he reacted to his brother. It was a weakness he could not afford. Besides which, Dorrek *had* taken up arms against Klag, and had disobeyed an instruction from his older brother—from the head of their House. Dorrek had joined forces with an enemy of their House. In truth, there could be only one solution.

Klag crossed his arms at the wrist in front of his face, his fingers clenched into fists. "You are cast out of the House of M'Raq, Dorrek. You have no claim to our lands, no House or father to call your own. You are discommendated, and I will no longer speak to you as brother."

With that, he cut off the communication. Dorrek's shocked face faded from the viewer.

Kurak was working on her eighth mug of *warnog* when she decided to contact Moloj on the Homeworld. She had never contacted Moloj herself. Indeed, she could not recall ever contacting any member of her House.

Then again, after seven and a half *warnogs*, she could barely recall the *name* of her House.

When Moloj's ugly face showed up on the viewer in her quarters, Kurak laughed. It was a long, tittery laugh, very unlike the one she used when she was sober—on those rare occasions that she *did* laugh when she was sober, in any event. Moloj had obviously been woken out of a sound sleep, and was in his nightclothes. Kurak had never imagined that Moloj even owned nightclothes, mainly because the very notion of him ever sleeping was one she could not wrap her mind around. Moloj was not one who would indulge in such niceties as *sleep.*...

"*What do you want, Kurak?*" Moloj said by way of greeting.

"Where is Gevnar?"

"*In his bed asleep—as I was. Are you drunk?*"

Again, she tittered. It was a most un-Klingonlike noise, and she supposed she should have been ashamed of it, but she didn't care. "Very. It was the only way to actually convince myself to go to the distasteful extreme of willingly speaking to you." She barked another laugh that was closer to her sober one. "Though it was worth it all to see you like this."

"*Why do you care where Gevnar is?*"

Kurak leaned forward, her head almost hitting the screen of the viewer. "Listen to me *very* very very carefully, Moloj. You are to hire a bodyguard for him. Find some Defense Force soldier who needs quick cash, there must be dozens of them hanging around the taverns in the First City. But I want him protected day and night. *No* harm must come to him, do you understand me?"

Moloj sighed dismissively. "*Kurak, you are inebriated, and I will not listen to your ramblings when—*"

Slamming her fist down on her workstation, Kurak bellowed, "I may not be the head of our House, but I am by Kahless the Lady of the House of

Palkar, and you *will* obey me, *gIntaq,* or I will have you killed in the middle of the Great Hall! Is that *understood?*"

Her door chime rang. She ignored it. Moloj stared at her with his mouth hanging open, a look of stupefaction that she had never seen on the old man's ugly visage.

"Is—that—understood?" she asked again.

"It will be as you say, Commander," Moloj said with as much respect as he was probably capable of dredging up.

"Good." The door chime rang again. Again, she ignored it. "If anything—*anything*—happens to that boy before he goes to officer training, I will hold you personally responsible, Moloj."

Before Moloj could say anything in response to that, Kurak cut the communication off. She could no longer stand to look at his face.

For a third time, the door chime rang. Finally she said, "Enter!"

The door rumbled open to reveal Leskit.

"Speaking of faces I can no longer stand to look at," she said, then gulped down the rest of her *warnog.* Or, rather, she tipped the mug toward her mouth, and most of it actually made it to her gullet.

"This is a sight I never thought I'd see." Leskit entered her cabin with a slight limp. She recalled dimly that Leskit had been injured during the battle, which was what caused Kornan to take over his position, and eventually be killed.

"Me drunk? Well, you should get used to it. I've found I enjoy it. Besides, it seems the best way to deal with this nightmare." She poured some more *warnog*, trying to recall of this was her eighth, ninth, or tenth mug. "Since commencing this obscene mission I have had my career threatened, lost the one thing I truly could call my own, and—probably something else, too, but I can't remember it. Getting drunk seemed the right thing to do." She looked over at Leskit. "Wait a minute. What are you doing here, Leskit? Why did I let you in?"

Leskit laughed. "Only you can answer that one, Kurak. However, I came here—and this will make you laugh—"

"I doubt it." She didn't find Leskit at all funny, even if he did make her laugh. Sometimes. She took another swig of *warnog*.

"I came here to share a drink with you."

Against her better judgment, Kurak laughed. The laugh started in her left stomach and exploded upward through her body and out her mouth. She couldn't stop it. She tried to, but her resistance was low from all however-many *warnog*s she'd had. So she continued to laugh. When she ran out of breath, she choked a bit, coughed, then laughed some more.

By the time the laugh finally died down, she realized that she was on her bunk, Leskit sitting next to her, laughing just as hard.

"I told you it would make you laugh."

"Yes. Yes, you did. What you did not tell me is why."

"Why what?"

Kurak punched Leskit on the shoulder. "*Why* do you wish to share a drink with me?"

The smile fell from Leskit's face, and his voice became somber. "To salute Kornan."

Spitting on the floor—a difficult task, given how dehydrated the *warnog* had made her—Kurak said, "Why would I wish to drink to that *toDSaH*'s memory? He is one of the reasons why I have to drink now. His importuning and his threatening and his pathetic skills on the wind boat...."

Quietly, Leskit said, "Because he was my friend. And because there is no one else on this ship with whom I wish to share that drink."

All of a sudden, Kurak remembered why it was she had let Leskit into her bed months ago when they first served together on this ship—and also why she had steadfastly refused to invite him back. He was maddening, he was attractive, he was infuriating, he smelled wonderful, he drove her insane, he made her laugh.

Leskit got up from the bunk, grabbed two fresh mugs from the shelf on the far bulkhead, and poured from a bottle of bloodwine. Kurak hated bloodwine, but still took the mug from Leskit.

"To Kornan," Leskit said, holding his mug up. "He was a mediocre warrior, a terrible shot, and an awful *grinnak* player. But he was a good friend—and he died well." Then he drank down the bloodwine.

Kurak followed suit, not sure why she was doing so. The bloodwine tasted oily and repulsive, and mixed badly with the residue of *warnog* that was already in her mouth. "Why haven't I kicked you out of my cabin?" she asked him.

"I really cannot say," the pilot replied with a grin. "Perhaps it's my natural charm."

Growling, Kurak said, "That could hardly be the case. I hate bloodwine, I hate Kornan, and I hate you. I'm glad Kornan's dead, because it means he won't be bothering me anymore. Now I have to worry about Gevnar, and do you know what the worst thing is?"

"Who's Gevnar? Never mind," Leskit added quickly, "I don't want to know. What is the worst thing?"

"Captain Klag wanted to give me a *medal* for finding a way to get the disruptors to work!"

"I suspect our captain is giddy from his unexpected victory," Leskit said dryly. "But none of this answers your question. Why haven't you kicked me out?"

Kurak searched through her alcohol-soaked brain for an answer to that question.

Klag stood amid the trees of San-Tarah for the final time.

No, he thought, *not the final time. I will return to this place one day.*

Me-Larr and Te-Run approached him and Morr, who stood to the side, followed immediately by B'Oraq and one of the *Gorkon* troops—the Leader of Fifteenth Squad, based on the insignia on her biceps.

"Farewell, Captain Klag," Me-Larr said. "I am sorry that you and your ship cannot stay longer." He turned to B'Oraq. "Especially you, Doctor. We have learned much from your people, and it is my hope that we will learn a great deal more, but your healing arts have been especially valuable."

"Yes," B'Oraq said dryly, "I've found the one place that has medical practices even more appalling than that of the Klingon Empire."

"No longer," Klag said. "For San-Tarah is part of the Klingon Empire now."

"And needs just as much help." B'Oraq smiled. "I wish I could stay, Me-Larr, but my duty is to my ship and my captain. And I suspect that he will not let me shirk that duty so easily."

"Indeed he will not," Klag said with a laugh. "But I am sure that Governor Huss will do what she can to facilitate your ability to heal yourselves."

B'Oraq tugged on her braid. "Truly you are an innovator, Captain. Who else could find a world that the *Klingons* could bring improved medicine to?"

"You have brought us much more than that, Captain," Me-Larr said. "I meant my words to your Ruling Pack's leader. You have shown us the universe, and told us that it has others like us."

"True," Klag said, "but it has others who are not like us at all."

Te-Run said, "But they do not matter, for we now have the protection of the Klingon Empire."

"Indeed." He turned to the auburn-haired soldier. "Leader, inform *QaS DevwI'* Vok that I am ready to depart and that all *Gorkon* personnel are to return to the ship immediately."

"Yes, Captain," she said quickly. She turned to leave, then gave B'Oraq a look. "Thank you again, Doctor, for that confirmation." With that, she left.

That struck Klag as odd. "Confirmation?"

"It is a personal matter, Captain, and I can assure you it will have no bearing on Leader Wol's ability to perform her duties."

Anger filled Klag's heart. "That is *not* for you to judge, Doctor."

"If it makes you feel better, Captain, Lieutenant Lokor is aware of this matter as well. If it *does* become an issue, I am sure that he will deal with it—and inform you if necessary."

Klag seethed. On the one hand, he did not believe that troops should be discussing personal matters with the ship's doctor. On the other hand, he trusted both B'Oraq and Lokor. So he let it go. *I cannot manage every aspect of a ship of almost three thousand.*

"Good-bye, Captain Klag," Me-Larr said. "You shall always be welcome on San-Tarah. If you are able, we would be—honored if you would join us in the Great Hunt next season."

Klag smiled. "The honor will be mine. May you fight well, Me-Larr, and you as well, Te-Run. And when you do die, may you lead those who run with the dead."

Te-Run let out an odd noise, and Me-Larr said,

"That is not how our afterlife works, but we appreciate the thought."

Laughing, Klag said, "Well, our afterlife might well let your kind in, given your prowess in battle. I know that I would welcome you on *my* ship in *Sto-Vo-Kor*. *Qapla'*, Me-Larr."

"Good fighting, Captain Klag."

Then Klag ordered his new first officer to beam him, B'Oraq, and Morr back to the *Gorkon*. Upon arrival, he immediately went to the bridge, leaving the doctor to go back to the medical bay.

On the way, Klag said to Morr, "I wish to recommence our *bat'leth* drills, Morr."

"Yes, sir."

"And this time, do not go gently with me. I have a very long way to go before I have returned to my old prowess, and I will not be satisfied until such a time as I have achieved it. Is that understood, Morr?"

"Yes, sir."

Morr spoke with the blandness that any soldier would present to his captain. *Which I suppose is the best I can hope for.* "Good."

Klag moved toward his command chair. From the chair to his right, the *Gorkon*'s new first officer said, "Crew replacements have beamed over from the *Kreltek*, sir, and have been assigned duties. All personnel have transported from the surface. We are ready to depart on your order."

Turning to look at Toq, Klag said, "The order is given."

Commander Toq gave his captain a wide smile, one that shone as brightly as the new medal on his uniform that indicated his promotion. "Yes, *sir*. Leskit, set course 103 mark 22. Proceed at full impulse until we have cleared this system, then execute at warp four."

"Consider us proceeding, Commander," Leskit said with a smirk.

Toq turned to the new operations officer. "Prepare long-range sensors." He looked back at Klag. "We must find new worlds to conquer."

"Indeed we must, Commander. Indeed we must."

GLOSSARY OF KLINGON TERMS

Most of the language actually being spoken in this novel is in the Klingon tongue, and has been translated into English for the reader's ease. Some terms that don't have direct translations into English or are proper nouns of some kind have been left in the Klingon language. Since that language does not use the same alphabet as English, the transliterations of the Klingon terms vary depending on preference. In many cases, a more Anglicized transliteration is used instead of the *tlhIngan Hol* transliterations preferred by linguists (e.g., the more Anglicized *bat'leth* is preferred over the *tlhIngan Hol* spelling *betleH*).

Below is a glossary of the Klingon terms used. Anglicized spellings are in **boldface;** *tlhIngan Hol* transliterations are in **bold italics.** Please note that this glossary does not include the names of locations, people, or ships. Where applicable, episode, movie, or novel citations are given where the term first appeared. Episode citations are followed by an abbreviation indicating show: TNG=*Star Trek: The Next Generation*, DS9=*Star Trek: Deep Space Nine*.

bat'leth *(betleH)*

Curved, four-bladed, two-handed weapon. This is the most popular handheld, edged weapon used by Klingon warriors owing to its being favored by Kahless, who forged the first one. The legendary Sword of Kahless now held by Chancellor Martok is a *bat'leth*, and most Defense Force warriors are proficient in it. [First seen in "Reunion" (TNG).]

bekk *(beq)*

A rank given to enlisted personnel in the Defense Force. [First referenced in "Sons and Daughters" (DS9).]

bok-rat liver, stewed *(boqrat chej)*

Food made from the liver of a *bok-rat*, apparently cooked to some degree, making it unusual among Klingon foods. [First seen in "Soldiers of the Empire" (DS9).]

bolmaq

An animal native to the planet Boreth that makes a bleating sound and tends to run around in circles a lot.

d'k tahg *(Daqtagh)*

Personal dagger. Most Defense Force warriors carry their own *d'k tahg*; higher-born Klingons often have them personalized with their name and House. [First seen in *Star Trek III: The Search for Spock*.]

gIntaq

A type of spear with a wooden haft and a curved,

two-bladed metal point. Also the name given to a person who serves as a close and trusted advisor to a House. It is possible that the latter usage evolved from the first, with the advisor being analogized to a House Head's trusted weapon. Sometimes Anglicized as *gin'tak*. [Spear first seen in "Birthright Part 2" (TNG); advisor first referenced in "Firstborn" (TNG).]

glob fly *(ghIlab ghew)*

Small, irritating insect with no sting and which makes a slight buzzing sound. [First referenced in "The Outrageous Okona" (TNG).]

Gre'thor *(ghe'tor)*

The afterlife for the dishonored dead—the closest Klingon equivalent to hell. Those who are unworthy spend eternity riding the Barge of the Dead to *Gre'thor*. [First mentioned in "Devil's Due" (TNG).]

grinnak *(ghInaq)*

A game.

grishnar cat *(ghISnar)*

Small animal, apparently not a very vicious one, though with perhaps a predilection for trying to sound fiercer than it actually is. [First referenced in "The Way of the Warrior" (DS9).]

Hem

Pride, to be proud.

jatyIn

According to legend, spirits of the dead that possess the living. [First mentioned in "Power Play" (TNG).]

jeghpu'wI'

Conquered people—more than slaves, less than

citizens, this status is given to the natives of worlds conquered by the Klingon Empire. [First used in *Diplomatic Implausibility*.]

klongat *(tlhongaD)*

A beast native to Qo'noS that is much larger than a *targ* and more difficult to subdue.

loSmaH Soch

The number forty-seven.

Mauk-to'Vor *(ma' to'vor)*

A death ritual that allows one who has lost honor to die well and go to *Sto-Vo-Kor* by being honorably killed by a Housemate or someone equally close. [First seen in "Sons of Mogh" (DS9).]

mek'leth *(meqleH)*

A swordlike one-handed weapon about half the size of a *bat'leth*. [First seen in "Sons of Mogh" (DS9).]

mok'bara *(moqbara)*

Martial art that focuses both the body and the spirit. [First seen in "Man of the People" (TNG).]

ngIS

Lubricant used on disruptor cannons.

petaQ

Insult with no direct translation. Sometimes anglicized as *pahtk*. [First used in "The Defector" (TNG).]

Qapla'

Ritual greeting that literally means "success." [First used in *Star Trek III: The Search for Spock*.]

QaS DevwI'

Troop commander on a Defense Force vessel, generally in charge of several dozen soldiers. Roughly analogous to a sergeant in the modern-day army. [First used in *The Brave & the Bold* Book 2.]

qelI'qam

Unit of measurement roughly akin to two kilometers. Sometimes anglicized as *kellicam*. [First used in *Star Trek III: The Search for Spock*.]

QI'yaH

Interjection with no direct translation. [First used in "Sins of the Father" (TNG).]

qutluch

A weapon favored by assassins, one that leaves a particularly vicious wound. [First seen in "Sins of the Father" (TNG).]

Qu'vatlh

Interjection with no direct translation.

racht (raHta')

Food made from live serpent worms (not to be confused with *gagh*). [First seen in "Melora" (DS9).]

raktajino (ra'taj)

Coffee, Klingon style. [First seen in "The Passenger" (DS9).]

ramjep bird

Avian life-form indigenous to Qo'noS that comes out only in the dark, and is sometimes served as food. Name literally means "midnight." [First referenced in *Diplomatic Implausibility*.]

Sto-Vo-Kor (Suto'vo'qor)

The afterlife for the honored dead, where all true warriors go, crossing the River of Blood after they die to fight an eternal battle. The closest Klingon equivalent to heaven. [First mentioned by name in "Rightful Heir" (TNG).]

taknar *(taqnar)*

An animal, the gizzards of which are sometimes served as food. [First referenced in *A Good Day to Die*.]

targ *(targh)*

Animal that is popular as a pet, but the heart of which is also considered a delicacy. [First seen as a pet in "Where No One Has Gone Before" (TNG) and as a food in "A Matter of Honor" (TNG).]

tik'leth *(tIqleH)*

An edged weapon, similar to an Earth longsword. [First seen in "Reunion" (TNG).]

toDSaH

Insult with no direct translation. Sometimes anglicized as *tohzah*. [First used in "The Defector" (TNG).]

trigak *(tlhIghaq)*

A predatory animal with sharp teeth that it bares before attacking.

vagh

The number five.

vIHbe'

A paralyzing poison that leaves no trace. Word literally means "not move."

wej

The number three.

yIntagh

Epithet with no direct translation. [First used in *A Good Day to Die*.]

ACKNOWLEDGMENTS

The sheer tonnage of people who need to be thanked for the existence of these two books (and this series) is vast enough to challenge the cargo capacity of the *Gorkon* itself, so let's get started....

First of all, John J. Ordover of Pocket Books, who first said, "Okay" to the idea of creating a Klingon crew for *Diplomatic Implausibility*, then said, "Why don't we do a series of *Gorkon* books?" after *DI* came out. Thanks also to Carol Greenburg, line editor extraordinaire; Paula M. Block, licensing goddess; John Van Citters, licensing god; and the other Pocket Books folks: Marco Palmieri, Jessica McGivney, Scott Shannon, Margaret Clark, John Perrella, and Elisa Kassin.

Any book based on a TV show takes its cues from the actors who played the roles. They're the ones who provide the voices you use to write the dialogue. With that in mind, loud kudos to Brian Thompson (who played Klag in *TNG*'s "A Matter of Honor"), Rick Worthy (Kornan in *DS9*'s "Soldiers of the Empire"), Sterling Macer Jr. (Toq in *TNG*'s "Birthright Part 2"), Tony Todd (Rodek in *DS9*'s "Sons of Mogh"), the late David Graf (Leskit in "Soldiers of the Empire"), Tricia O'Neill (Kurak in *TNG*'s "Suspicions"), Stephen Root (K'Vada in *TNG*'s "Unification Parts 1–2"), Laura Drake (Vekma in "A Matter of Honor"), and, of course, J.G. Hertzler (Martok) and Michael Dorn (Worf). Additional thanks to Keith Hamilton Cobb (best known as Tyr Anasazi on *Gene Roddenberry's Andromeda*), who served as the template for Lokor, and the late André the Giant, whose portrayal of Fezzick in *The Princess Bride* was the primary inspiration for Goran.

I must also profusely thank Wanda M. Haight, Gregory Amos, and Burton Armus, who wrote "A Matter of Honor," which not only was the debut of the character of Klag, but which also provided the background with his father, which has been such an important part of the character as he's evolved over the course of four books.

It is possible to write a *Star Trek* novel without consulting any reference material, but it isn't advised. *The Star Trek Encyclopedia* by Mike & Denise Okuda, with Debbie Mirek, the Okudas' *Star Trek Chronology*, *Star Charts* by Geoffrey Mandel, *The Starfleet Survival Guide* by David Mack, and the *Star Trek: The Next Generation Companion* and *Star Trek: Deep Space Nine Companion* CD-ROMs were all invaluable tools, as was *The Star Trek: Deep Space Nine Companion* book by Terry J. Erdmann & Paula M. Block (unrelated to the CD). Man-Fai Wan's Ships of the Starfleet Web site (manfai.wan.users.btopenworld.com) was inordinately helpful. And, of course, one cannot forget *The Klingon Dictionary* by Marc Okrand, as well as all the supplemental help from Marc and Dr. Lawrence Schoen of the Klingon Language Institute (www.kli.org).

Huge dollops of thanks go to Dayton Ward, who is both an ex-Marine and a fine science fiction author in his own right, and who helped me keep my military strategy straight. Any screwups of same are entirely the fault of the civilian author.

Tammy Love Larrabee took the vague idea of what the *Qang*-class (Chancellor-class) ships in general and the *Gorkon* in particular looked like in my head and created a wonderful set of specs for them, which can be found in the back of *The Brave and the Bold* Book 2 (and which also served as the basis for the rendering of the *Gorkon* on the cover of *A Good Day to Die*). Tammy also wrote the House of Jakvi epigraph used in *A Good Day to Die*.

The late Hilary J. Bader wrote the "Warrior's Anthem," and was responsible for some damn fine genre television before ovarian cancer took her away far far too young. She passed away while I was writing Book 1, and she is sorely missed. Thanks also to René Echevarria, who wrote the victory song "Don't Speak," used in Chapter 12 of *A Good Day to Die*, for the episode "Birthright Part 2," and to Heather Jarman for writing the *Burning Hearts of Qo'noS* excerpt in Chapter 9 of *Honor Bound* for the novel *This Gray Spirit* (an excellent book that you should all go out and buy right now).

In addition to the previous two appearances of the I.K.S. *Gorkon* in *Diplomatic Implausibility* and *The Brave and the Bold* Book 2, this book also builds on the excellent story told by J.G. Hertzler and Jeffrey Lang in the *Star Trek: Deep Space Nine* duology *The Left Hand of Destiny*, and if you haven't picked them up yet, I strongly recommend you do so. They aren't necessary to follow the action of these two books, but they add to the experience, and besides, they're damn fine books that anyone who likes Klingons (or just generally a good epic yarn) will enjoy immensely.

Thanks also to: CITH, the best writers group in the whole history of the whole history, who again reached into my brain and yanked a better piece of fiction out of it than what I would've written on my own; GraceAnne Andreassi DeCandido, a.k.a. The Mom, for her usual editorial niftiness; the usual gang of idiots in the Geek Patrol and the Malibu crowd (you know who you are); the Magical Starbucks of Good Writing in midtown Manhattan (the staff of which has come to know me as "the root beer guy"); and the ever-supportive posters at various places online: Psi Phi's *Star Trek* Books BBS (www.psiphi.org), the *Trek* Literature Board at the *Trek* BBS (www.trekbbs.com), the *Star Trek* Books Board at SimonSays.com (www.startrekbooks.com), the "Divine Treasury" board at *Trek* Web (www.trekweb.com), the Federation Library at *Star Trek* Now! (www.startreknow.com), and the *Star Trek* Books YahooGroup (groups.yahoo.com).

As always, though, the biggest thanks go to my *par'machkai* Terri Osborne, as well as to our cats, Mittens and Marcus, who have never failed to provide me with large amounts of love, affection, and support.

ABOUT THE AUTHOR

Keith R.A. DeCandido has written a wide variety of *Star Trek* material in an equally wide variety of media: novels, short fiction, comic books, and eBooks. That material includes the *Star Trek: The Next Generation* novel *Diplomatic Implausibility* (which introduced the *I.K.S. Gorkon*), the *Star Trek: Deep Space Nine* novel *Demons of Air and Darkness* and the followup novella "Horn and Ivory" in *What Lay Beyond* (both part of the ongoing series of post-finale *DS9* stories), *Star Trek: The Brave & the Bold* (a two-book series that covered all five TV shows and also included Captain Klag and the *Gorkon*), the TNG comic book *Perchance to Dream*, the novel *The Art of the Impossible* (part of the *Star Trek The Lost Era* miniseries), the *DS9* short story "Broken Oaths" in the *Prophecy and Change* anthology, the *Star Trek: New Frontier* short story "Revelations" in the *No Limits* anthology, and several *Star Trek: S.C.E.* eBooks (a monthly series co-developed by

About the Author

Keith of adventures featuring the Starfleet Corps of Engineers; the first sixteen have been reprinted in the volumes *Have Tech, Will Travel; Miracle Workers; Some Assembly Required;* and *No Surrender*). Forthcoming forays into the *Star Trek* universe include *Tales of the Dominion War* (an anthology of short stories edited by Keith, due in the summer of 2004), a two-book *Star Trek: The Next Generation* story focusing on Ambassador Worf in the time leading up to *Star Trek Nemesis*, further adventures in the worlds of *Deep Space Nine*, and more tales of the *I.K.S. Gorkon*.

Keith—whose work has been praised by *Entertainment Weekly*, TrekNation.com, *TV Zone*, Cinescape.com, *Dreamwatch*, and *Publishers Weekly*, among others—has also written novels, short stories, and nonfiction books in the universes of *Buffy the Vampire Slayer*, *Gene Roddenberry's Andromeda*, *Farscape*, *Doctor Who*, *Xena*, Marvel Comics, and more. He is the editor of the groundbreaking *Imaginings: An Anthology of Long Short Fiction*, his original novel, *Dragon Precinct*, will be published in 2004, and his original short fiction can be found in *Murder by Magick*, *Urban Nightmares*, and *Did You Say Chicks!?* Keith, who is also a musician and an avid New York Yankees fan, lives in the Bronx with his girlfriend and the world's two goofiest cats. Learn too much about Keith at his official Web site at DeCandido.net, join his fan club at KRADfanclub.com, or just send him silly e-mails at keith@decandido.net.

Look for STAR TREK fiction from Pocket Books

Star Trek®

Novelizations
Star Trek books by William Shatner with Judith and Garfield Reeves-Stevens

Star Trek®: The Original Series

Star Trek: The Next Generation®

Novelizations

Trials and Tribble-ations • Diane Carey
Far Beyond the Stars • Steve Barnes
What You Leave Behind • Diane Carey

#1 • Emissary • J.M. Dillard
#2 • The Siege • Peter David
#3 • Bloodletter • K.W. Jeter
#4 • The Big Game • Sandy Schofield
#5 • Fallen Heroes • Dafydd ab Hugh
#6 • Betrayal • Lois Tilton
#7 • Warchild • Esther Friesner
#8 • Antimatter • John Vornholt
#9 • Proud Helios • Melissa Scott
#10 • Valhalla • Nathan Archer
#11 • Devil in the Sky • Greg Cox & John Gregory Betancourt
#12 • The Laertian Gamble • Robert Sheckley
#13 • Station Rage • Diane Carey
#14 • The Long Night • Dean Wesley Smith & Kristine Kathryn
  Rusch
#15 • Objective: Bajor • John Peel
#16 • Invasion! #3: Time's Enemy • L.A. Graf
#17 • The Heart of the Warrior • John Gregory Betancourt
#18 • Saratoga • Michael Jan Friedman
#19 • The Tempest • Susan Wright
#20 • Wrath of the Prophets • David, Friedman & Greenberger
#21 • Trial by Error • Mark Garland
#22 • Vengeance • Dafydd ab Hugh
#23 • The 34th Rule • Armin Shimerman & David R. George III
#24-26 • Rebels • Dafydd ab Hugh
  #24 • The Conquered
  #25 • The Courageous
  #26 • The Liberated

Books set after the series
  The Lives of Dax • Marco Palmieri, ed.
  Millennium Omnibus • Judith and Garfield Reeves-Stevens
    #1 • The Fall of Terok Nor
    #2 • The War of the Prophets
    #3 • Inferno
  A Stitch in Time • Andrew J. Robinson
  Avatar, Books One and Two • S.D. Perry
  Section 31: Abyss • David Weddle & Jeffrey Lang
  Gateways #4: Demons of Air and Darkness • Keith R.A. DeCandido
  Gateways #7: What Lay Beyond: "Horn and Ivory" • Keith R.A.
    DeCandido

Books set after the series
    Homecoming • Christie Golden
    The Farther Shore • Christie Golden

Enterprise®

Novelizations
    Broken Bow • Diane Carey
    Shockwave • Paul Ruditis
    The Expanse • J.M. Dillard
By the Book • Dean Wesley Smith & Kristine Kathryn Rusch
What Price Honor? • Dave Stern
Surak's Soul • J.M. Dillard
Daedalus • Dave Stern

Star Trek: New Frontier®

New Frontier #1-4 Collector's Edition • Peter David
    #1 • House of Cards
    #2 • Into the Void
    #3 • The Two-Front War
    #4 • End Game
#5 • Martyr • Peter David
#6 • Fire on High • Peter David
The Captain's Table #5 • Once Burned • Peter David
Double Helix #5 • Double or Nothing • Peter David
#7 • The Quiet Place • Peter David
#8 • Dark Allies • Peter David
#9-11 • Excalibur • Peter David
    #9 • Requiem
    #10 • Renaissance
    #11 • Restoration
Gateways #6: Cold Wars • Peter David
Gateways #7: What Lay Beyond: "Death After Life" • Peter David
#12 • Being Human • Peter David
#13 • Gods Above • Peter David
#14 • Stone and Anvil • Peter David
No Limits • Peter David, ed.

Star Trek®: Stargazer

The Valiant • Michael Jan Friedman
Double Helix #6: The First Virtue • Michael Jan Friedman and Christie
    Golden
Gauntlet • Michael Jan Friedman
Progenitor • Michael Jan Friedman

STAR TREK

STARGAZER: OBLIVION

MICHAEL JAN FRIEDMAN

In 1893, a time-traveling Jean-Luc Picard encountered a long-lived alien named Guinan, who was posing as a human to learn Earth's customs.

This is the story of a Guinan very different from the woman we think we know.

A Guinan who yearns for oblivion.

Available Now

STSO.01

STAR TREK

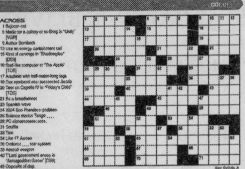

STAR TREK CROSSWORD SERIES

**50 ACROSS: Puzzles worked
on for amusement
CROSSWORDS
by *New York Times*
crossword puzzle
editor John Samson**

Available Now!

STCR.01